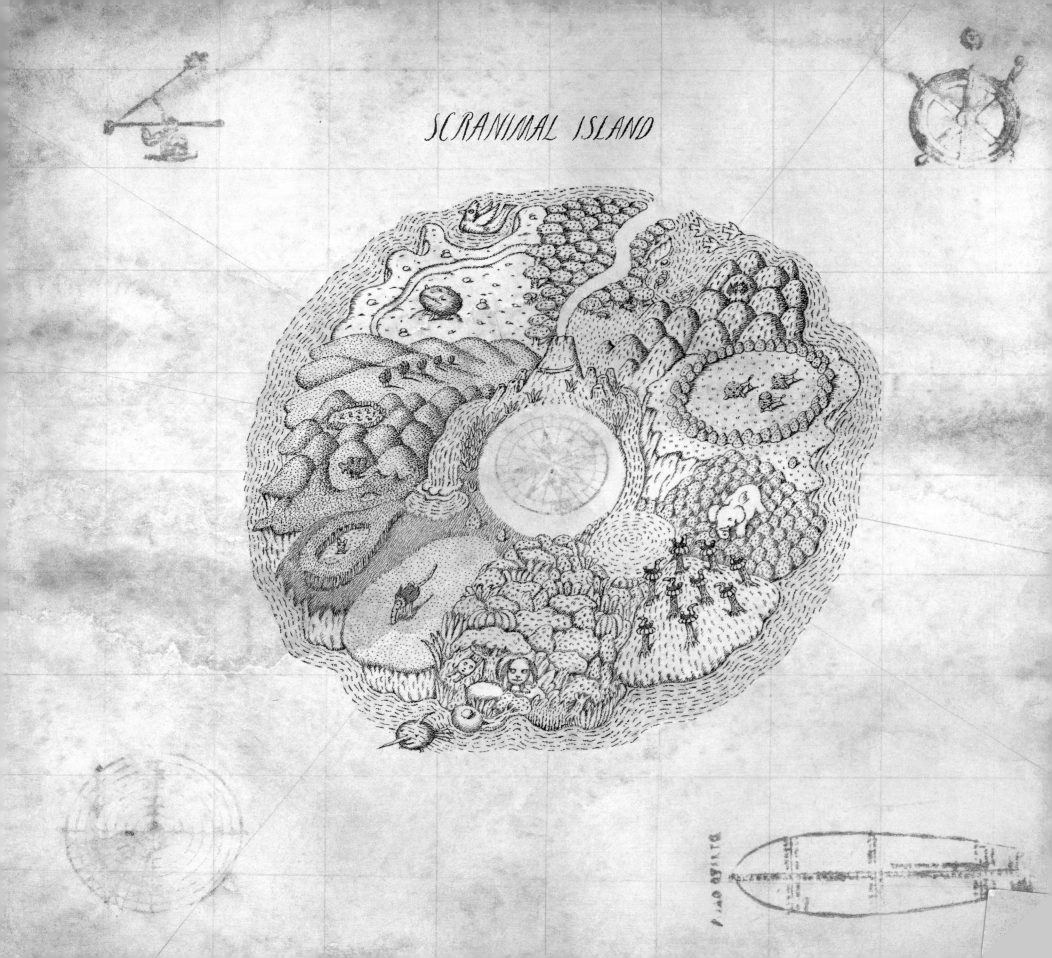

Scranimals

POEMS BY **JACK PRELUTSKY**

PICTURES BY **PETER SÍS**

GREENWILLOW BOOKS
An Imprint of HarperCollinsPublishers

TO AVA WEISS,
FOR BEAUTIFUL BOOKS
— J. P.

FOR GINNY MOORE KRUSE
AND EVERYONE AT THE
COOPERATIVE CHILDREN'S BOOK CENTER
— P. S.

Scranimals
Text copyright © 2002 by Jack Prelutsky
Illustrations copyright © 2002 by Peter Sís
All rights reserved.
Manufactured in China.

Black line art is combined with watercolors for the full-color illustrations.
The typeface is Gill Sans.

Library of Congress Cataloging-in-Publication Data

Prelutsky, Jack.
Scranimals / by Jack Prelutsky ; illustrated by Peter Sís.
     p.   cm.
"Greenwillow Books."
ISBN-10: 0-688-17819-7 (trade bdg.) — ISBN-13: 978-0-688-17819-2 (trade bdg.)
ISBN-10: 0-688-17820-0 (lib. bdg.) — ISBN-13: 978-0-688-17820-8 (lib. bdg.)
ISBN-10: 0-06-075368-4 (pbk.) — ISBN-13: 978-0-06-075368-9 (pbk.)
1. Nonsense-verses, American. 2. Children's poetry, American.
[1. Animals—Poetry. 2. Humorous poetry. 3. American poetry.]
I. Sís, Peter, ill. II. Title.   PS3566.R36 S37 2002
811'.54—dc21   2001023620

First Edition 09 10 11 12 13 SCP 10 9 8 7 6 5

CONTENTS

THE JOURNEY 5

OH BEAUTIFUL RHINOCEROSE 7

A CLUTCH OF SPINACHICKENS 9

THE CAMELBERTA PEACHES 11

THE POTATOAD 12

THE CARDINALBACORE 14

THE HIPPOPOTAMUSHROOMS 16

THE PARROTTERS 19

SWEET PORCUPINEAPPLE 21

A PRIDE OF BROCCOLIONS 22

THE PONDEROUS STORMY PETRELEPHANT 25

THE LOVELY TOUCANEMONES 26

THE DETESTED RADISHARK 29

OH SLEEK BANANACONDA 31

THERE! 32

BEHOLD THE OSTRICHEETAH 35

ON A CERTAIN MOUNTAIN MEADOW 36

POOR AVOCADODOS 39

THE RETURN 40

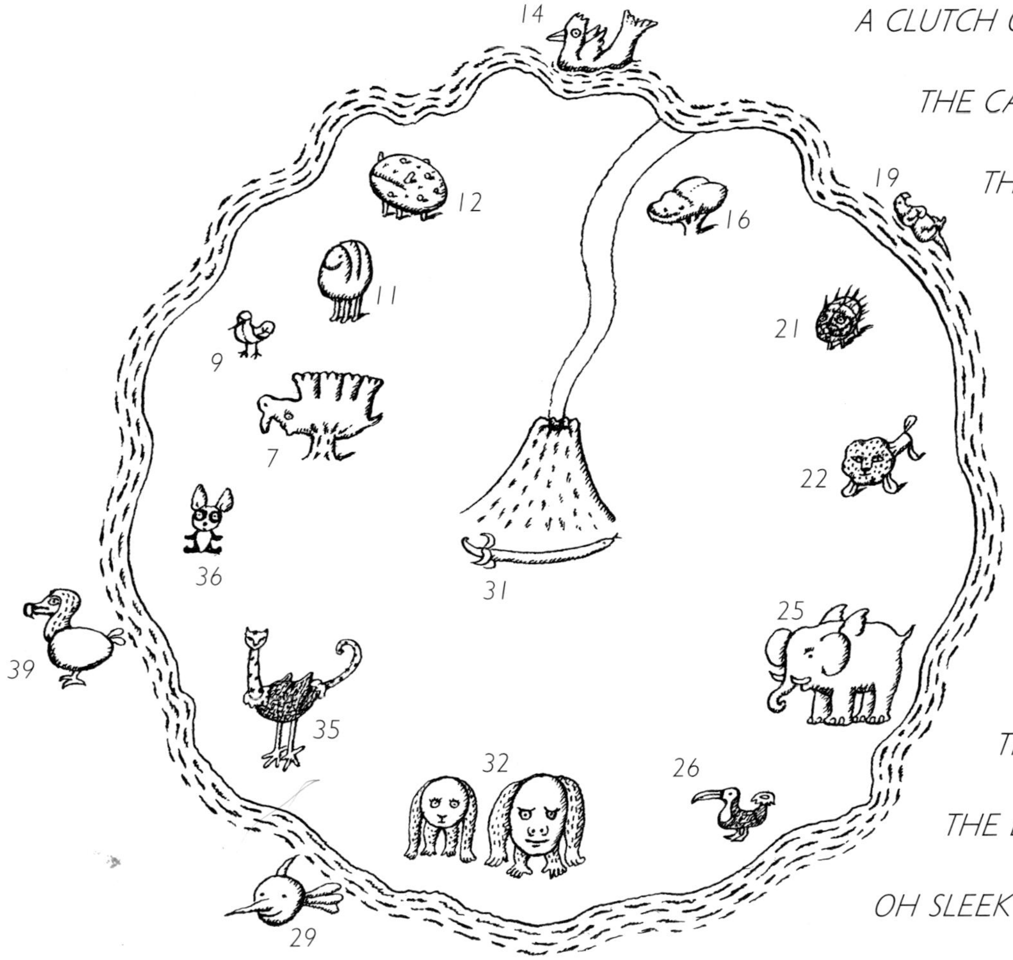

We're sailing to Scranimal Island,

It doesn't appear on most maps.

The PARROTTERS float on the tide there,

The STORMY PETRELEPHANT flaps.

We may find a rare OSTRICHEETAH,

There's never been one in a zoo.

We're sailing to Scranimal Island—

You're welcome to come along too.

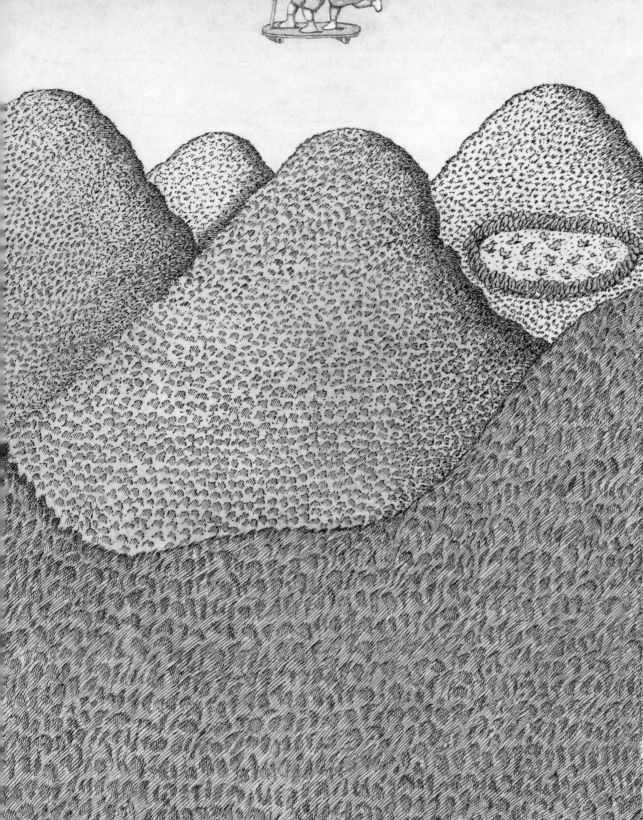

Oh beautiful RHINOCEROSE,
So captivating, head to toes,
So aromatic, toes to head,
Enchantress of the flower bed,
Your blossoms cheer us every morn,
And we adore your tail and horn.
You soothe the eyes, delight the nose,
Most glorious RHINOCEROSE.

rye-NOSS-ur-oze

Aclutch of SPINACHICKENS
Is fussing in the yard,
They peck their meager pickings,
Their lives are dull and hard.
Except for paltry feathers,
They're mostly leafy green,
Their heads are smooth as leather,
Their brains are not too keen.

Some say that they're distasteful,
While others think they're sweet,
They're never very graceful,
They wilt at signs of heat.
They mill about all morning
Upon their scrawny legs,
Then cluck a single warning
And lay their turquoise eggs.

spin-itch-ICK-inz

On the sunbaked, barren beaches,
Courtly **CAMELBERTA PEACHES**
Gather into stately bands
To patrol the burning sands.
Some are yellow, some are green,
Most are sort of in-between,
All have puffy, plump physiques,
Knobby knees, and fuzzy cheeks.

All have humpy, bumpy backs,
Stocked with water, juice, and snacks,
So the creatures never need
Wonder where to drink or feed.
By the salty sea they stride,
Never noticing the tide,
Up and down the sifting sands . . .
CAMELBERTA caravans.

CAM-ull-BURR-tuh

On a bump beside a road
Sits a lowly POTATOAD,
Obviously unaware
Of its own existence there.

On its coarse and warty hide,
It has eyes on every side,
Eyes that fail, apparently,
To take note of what they see.

It does not move, it does not think,
It does not eat, it does not drink,
It does not hear or taste or touch...
The POTATOAD does not do much.

The day is hot, the ground is parched,
And yet it sits as if it's starched.
To pose immobile by a road
Suffices for the POTATOAD.

poe-tay-TOAD

The CARDINALBACORE
Has a face entirely red.
Its busy wings are sore
From holding up its head.
It hovers on the brink,
Its existence isn't fair,
Its tail flops in the drink,
But its top stays in the air.

It simply cannot let
Its own bottom pull it down.
If it got entirely wet,
It would definitely drown.
Yet the CARDINALBACORE
Seems undaunted by the fact
That its life is nothing more
Than a full-time circus act.

car-din-AL-buh-core

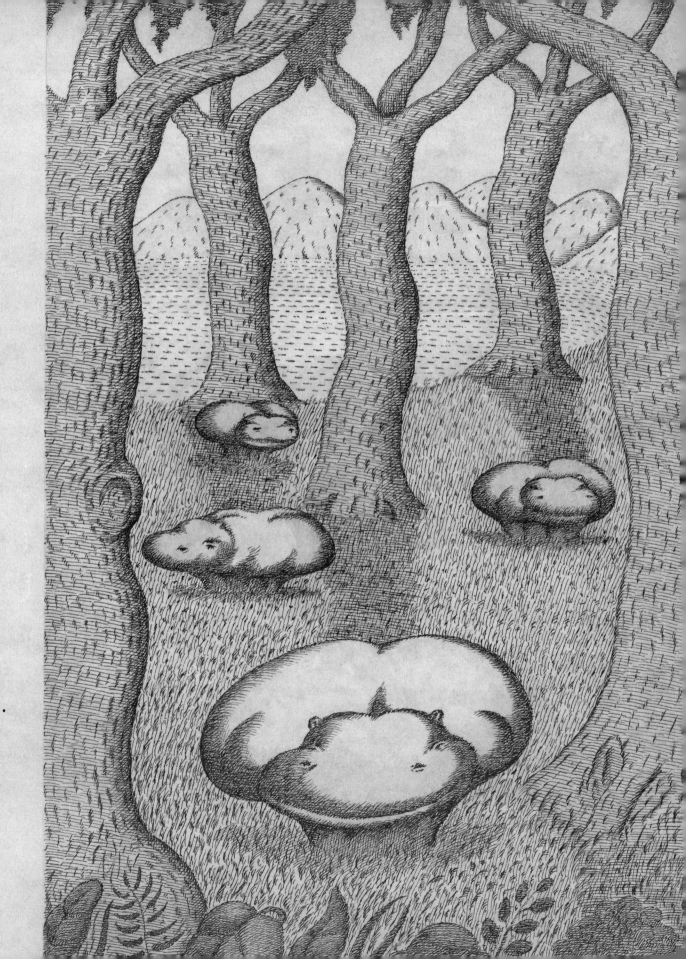

The HIPPOPOTAMUSHROOMS
Cannot wander very far.
How fortunate they're satisfied
Precisely where they are.
They feel no need to travel,
They're forever at their ease,
Relaxing on the forest floor
Beneath the shady trees.

The HIPPOPOTAMUSHROOMS
Suffer from deficient grace,
And their tubby, blobby bodies
Tend to take up too much space.
But they compensate with manners
For the things they lack in style...
They are models of politeness,
And they always wear a smile.

hip-uh-pot-uh-MUSH-rooms

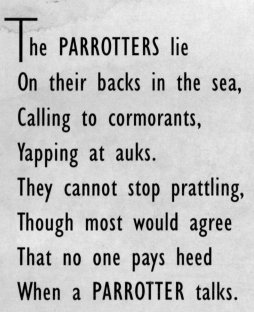

The **PARROTTERS** lie
On their backs in the sea,
Calling to cormorants,
Yapping at auks.
They cannot stop prattling,
Though most would agree
That no one pays heed
When a **PARROTTER** talks.

PAA-rot-urz

Sweet PORCUPINEAPPLE,
Unflappable chap,
You happily amble
All over the map.
Sharp prickles protect
Your subtropical hide,
Not many could chew you,
Not many have tried.

Your spirits are high,
And your worries are few,
You go where you go,
And you do what you do.
A pointed example
Of perfect design,
Sweet PORCUPINEAPPLE,
Your life is divine.

por-cue-pie-NAP-ul

A pride of BROCCOLIONS
Has assembled in the grass,
Paying scrupulous attention
To the creatures ranging past.
Then an ANTELOPETUNIA
Moves directly into view,
And the chase begins in earnest,
And they all know what to do.

They are beasts of regal bearing
In their coats of green and gold.
They are fierce and prepossessing,
They are cunning, they are bold.
Soon their chosen victim stumbles,
For despite its nimble gait,
Its pursuers overtake it
And consign it to its fate.

With adroitness and precision
They dispatch their fallen prey,
And that ANTELOPETUNIA
Will not bloom another day.
Then that pride of BROCCOLIONS,
Having hunted, having fed,
Growls and yawns in satisfaction
And goes noisily to bed.

brock-uh-LIE-unz
an-till-oh-puh-TUNE-yuh

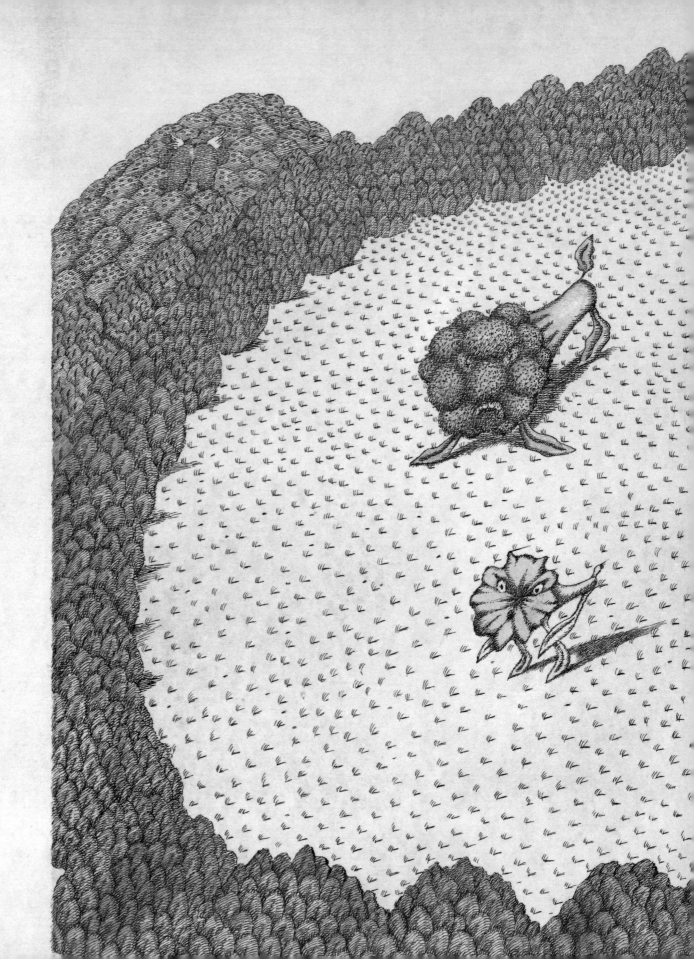

The ponderous **STORMY PETRELEPHANT**
Is futilely trying to fly.
Its efforts are clearly irrelevant,
One look and it's plain to see why.
Its wings are too small to support it,
They're patently only for show,
And so it is constantly thwarted . . .
Up isn't a place it can go.

It hasn't a hope of succeeding,
It's destined to wander the plains,
Which, given its bulk and its breeding,
Is where we prefer it remains.
The **STORMY PETRELEPHANT**'s failures
Relieve us of absolute dread.
We love it in fields of azaleas—
We'd hate if it soared overhead.

peh-TRELL-uh-fint

The lovely TOUCANEMONES,
Profuse upon the hills,
Display their gaudy petals
And their multicolored bills.
They revel in the sunshine,
They rejoice to feel the breeze,
And every drop of rain delights
The TOUCANEMONES.

The lovely TOUCANEMONES
Are quite a noisy bunch.
They chatter when they waken
And continue well past lunch.
If you should pet their blossoms,
Tantalizing to the touch,
They're apt to nip your fingers,
Though they will not nip them much.

At times the TOUCANEMONES
May flap their wings awhile,
As if to rise into the skies,
But that is not their style.
They're clearly underqualified
To soar above the trees—
An earthbound life's the limit
For the TOUCANEMONES.

two-can-EM-uh-neez

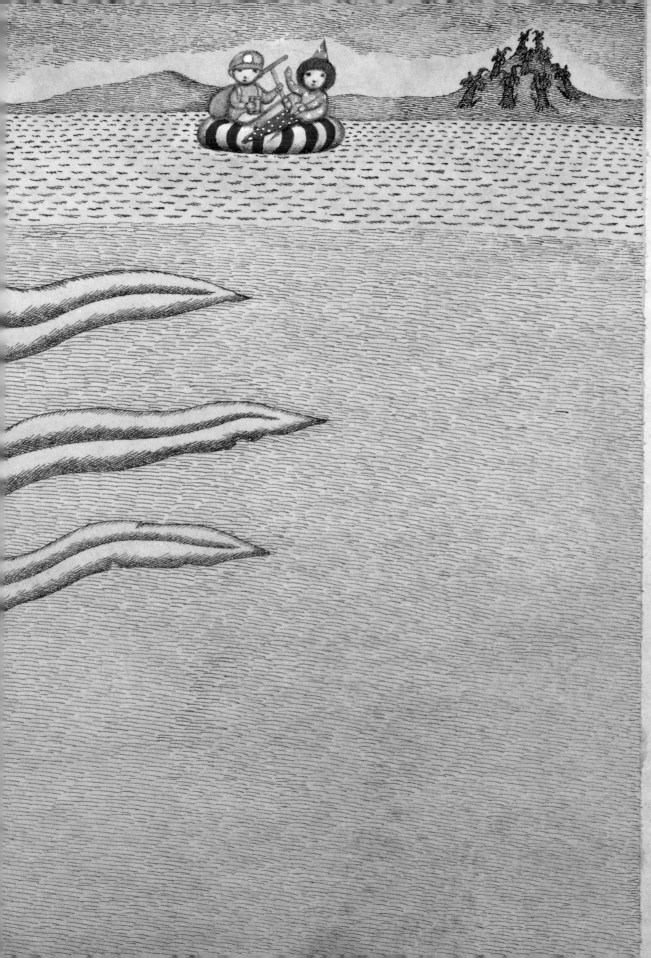

In the middle of the ocean,
In the deep deep dark,
Dwells a monstrous apparition,
The detested RADISHARK.
It's an underwater nightmare
That you hope you never meet,
For it eats what it wants,
And it always wants to eat.

Its appalling, bulbous body
Is astonishingly red,
And its fangs are sharp and gleaming
In its huge and horrid head,
And the only thought it harbors
In its small but frightful mind,
Is to catch you and to bite you
On your belly and behind.

It is ruthless, it is brutal,
It swims swiftly, it swims far,
So it's guaranteed to find you
Almost anywhere you are.
If the RADISHARK is near you,
Pray the beast is fast asleep
In the middle of the ocean
In the dark dark deep.

RAD-ish-ark

Oh sleek **BANANACONDA**,
You longest long long fellow,
How sinuous and sly you are,
How slippery, how yellow.

You slither on your belly,
And you slither on your chin.
You're only unappealing
As you shed your slinky skin.

buh-na-nuh-CON-duh

There! Cavorting through the jungle
In a sea of brilliant green,
Please observe the MANGORILLA
And ORANGUTANGERINE.
They are racing, they are sparring,
Playing leapfrog, tag, and catch,
And in every competition
They are one another's match.

Now the MANGORILLA dances
On a verdant, mossy bed,
While his acrobatic playmate
Swings in branches overhead.
We feel privileged to view them,
They are rare and seldom seen . . .
The enormous MANGORILLA,
The ORANGUTANGERINE.

man-guh-RILL-uh
uh-RANG-uh-tan-jur-EEN

Behold the OSTRICHEETAH,
A blur that rushes past,
There is not a creature fleeter,
Not a creature quite as fast.
It swiftly covers distance,
Never slackening its pace.
Throughout its whole existence,
It has yet to lose a race.

With fur and feathers flying,
It hurtles on and then,
Somehow, not even trying,
Accelerates again.
But when it tires of running,
It doesn't simply stand.
Though quick, it's far from cunning—
Its head goes in the sand.

ah-stri-CHEE-tuh

On a certain mountain meadow,
If you're silent, if you're still,
You may spy a single yellow,
Black, and white PANDAFFODIL.
You may even hear it yawning
If the morning's just begun,
Watch its petals slowly open
To embrace the rising sun.

You may see it soon meander
To a stand of tall bamboo,
Pluck a succulent example,
And commence to chomp and chew.
It may plop upon its belly,
Flop upon its downy back,
Turn an amiable cartwheel,
And continue with its snack.

You may see it fold its petals
When the sun sinks overhead,
And in languorous contentment
Trundle homeward and to bed.
You may never see another
Gentle, shy PANDAFFODIL,
Even on that mountain meadow,
Though you're silent, though you're still.

pan-DAFF-uh-dill

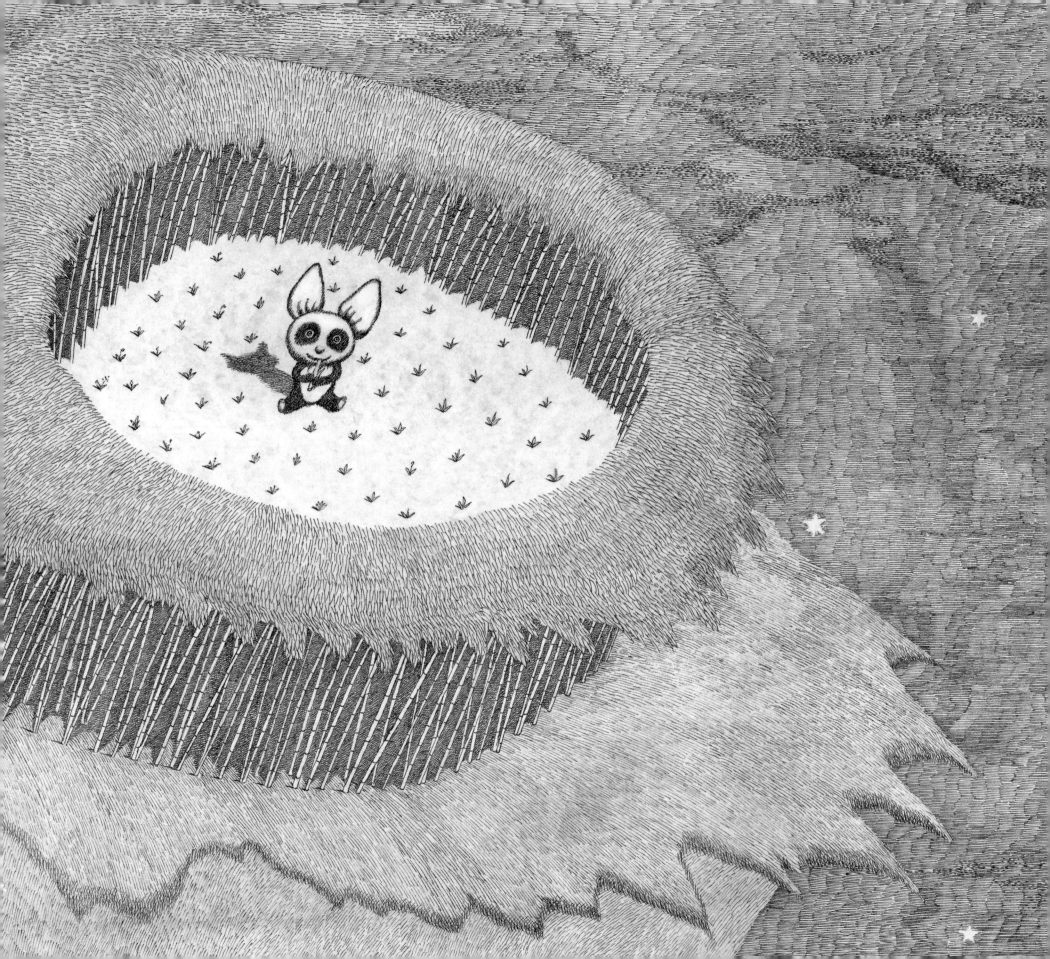

Poor AVOCADODOS,
Ungainly and green,
You're gone from today's
Biological scene.
Your craniums held
But a bit of brain,
Explaining in part
Why you didn't remain.

You never were fast,
And you never were strong,
It's hardly surprising
You couldn't last long.
A fruit and a fowl
Inexplicably linked,
Poor AVOCADODOS,
You're sadly extinct.

ah-vuh-ca-DOE-doze

We've journeyed to Scranimal Island,
Where magical creatures are found,
Where AVOCADODOS still flourish,
And green SPINACHICKENS abound.
We've seen a PANDAFFODIL dining,
A PORCUPINEAPPLE at play.
Perhaps there is more to discover—
We'd like to return there someday.

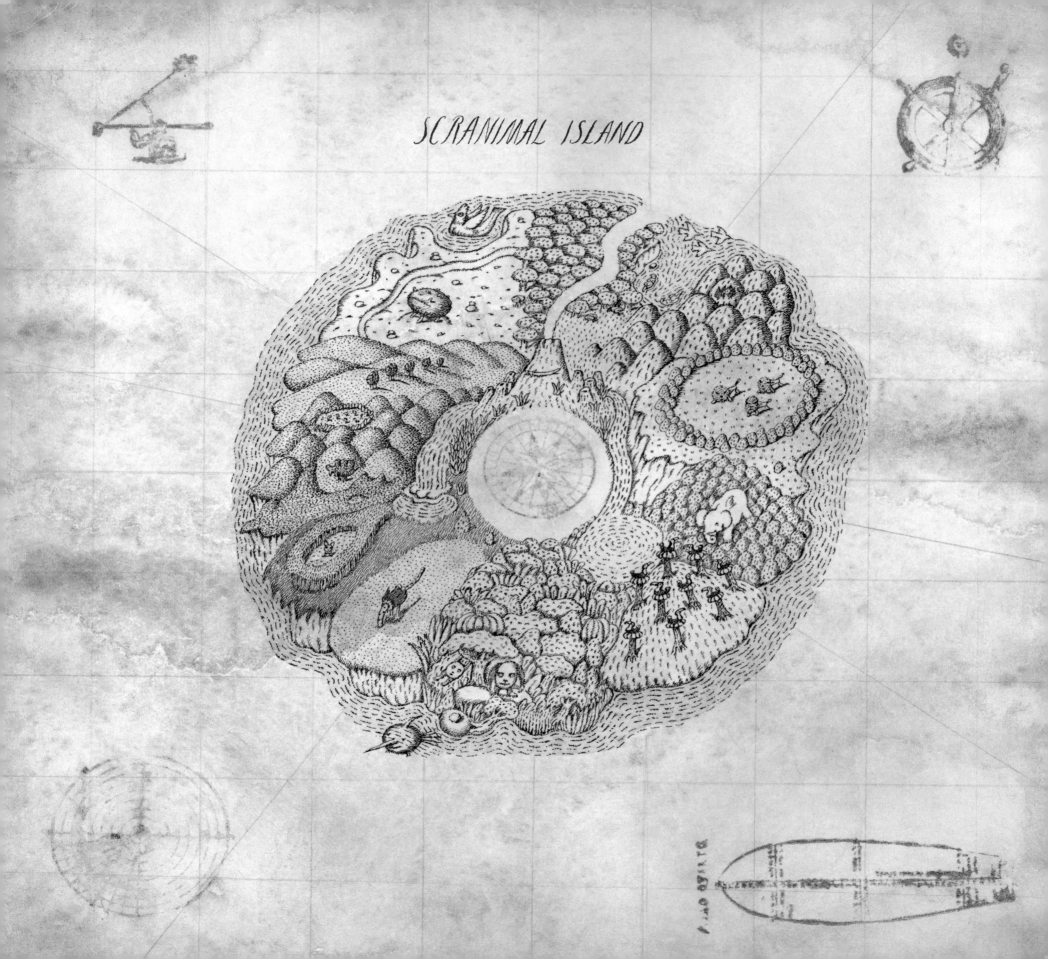

SUMMER BRAIN QUEST

Dear Parent,

At Brain Quest, we believe learning should be an adventure—a *quest* for knowledge. Our mission has always been to guide children on that quest, to keep them excited, motivated, and curious, and to give them the confidence they need to do well in school. Now, we're extending the quest to summer vacation! Meet SUMMER BRAIN QUEST: It's a workbook. It's a game. It's an outdoor adventure. And it's going to stop summer slide!

Research shows that if kids take a break from learning all summer, they can lose up to three months' worth of knowledge from the previous grade. So we set out to create a one-of-a-kind workbook experience that delivers personalized learning for every kind of kid. Personalized learning is an educational method where exercises are tailored to each child's strengths, needs, and interests. Our goal was to empower kids to have a voice in what and how they learned during the summer, while ensuring they get enough practice with the fundamentals. The result: SUMMER BRAIN QUEST—a complete interactive program that is easy to use and designed to engage each unique kid all summer long.

So how does it work? Each SUMMER BRAIN QUEST WORKBOOK includes a pullout tri-fold map that functions as a game board, progress chart, and personalized learning system. Our map shows different routes that correspond to over 100 pages of curriculum-based exercises and 8 outdoor learning experiences. The variety of routes enables kids to choose different topics and activities while guaranteeing practice in weaker skills. We've also included over 150 stickers to mark progress, incentivize challenging exercises, and celebrate accomplishments. As kids complete activities and earn stickers, they can put them wherever they like on the map, so each child's map is truly unique—just like your kid. To top it all off, we included a Summer Brainiac Award to mark your child's successful completion of his or her quest. SUMMER BRAIN QUEST guides kids so they feel supported, and it offers positive feedback and builds confidence by showing kids how far they've come and just how much they've learned.

Each SUMMER BRAIN QUEST WORKBOOK has been created in consultation with an award-winning teacher specializing in that grade. We cover the core competencies of reading, writing, and math, as well as the essentials of social studies and science. We ensure that our exercises are aligned to Common Core State Standards, Next Generation Science Standards, and state social studies standards.

Loved by kids and adored by teachers, Brain Quest is America's #1 educational bestseller and has been an important bridge to the classroom for millions of children. SUMMER BRAIN QUEST is an effective new tool for parents, homeschoolers, tutors, and teachers alike to stop summer slide. By providing fun, personalized, and meaningful educational materials, our mission is to help ALL kids keep their skills ALL summer long. Most of all, we want kids to know:

It's your summer. It's your workbook. It's your learning adventure.

—The editors of Brain Quest

This book belongs to:

_____

Library of Congress Cataloging-in-Publication Data is available.

ISBN 978-0-7611-8918-3

Summer Series Concept by Nathalie Le Du, Daniel Nayeri, Tim Hall
Writers   Persephone Walker, Claire Piddock
Consulting Editor   Jane Ching Fung
Art Director   Colleen AF Venable
Cover, Map, Sticker, and Additional Character Illustrator   Edison Yan
Illustrator   Matt Cummings
Series Designer   Tim Hall
Editor   Nathalie Le Du
Production Editor   Jessica Rozler
Production Manager   Julie Primavera

Workman books are available at special discounts when purchased in bulk for premiums and sales promotions as well as for fund-raising or educational use. Special editions or book excerpts can also be created to specification. For details, contact the Special Sales Director at the address below, or send an email to specialmarkets@workman.com.

DISCLAIMER
The publisher and authors disclaim responsibility for any loss, injury, or damages caused as a result of any of the instructions described in this book.

Workman Publishing Co., Inc.
225 Varick Street
New York, NY 10014-4381
workman.com

BRAIN QUEST, IT'S FUN TO BE SMART!, and WORKMAN are registered trademarks of Workman Publishing Co., Inc.

Printed in China
First printing March 2017

10 9 8 7 6 5 4 3 2 1

SUMMER BRAIN QUEST

BETWEEN GRADES 2 & 3

For adventurers ages 7–8

Written by Persephone Walker and Claire Piddock
Consulting Editor: Jane Ching Fung

WORKMAN PUBLISHING

NEW YORK

Contents

Instructions.................................5

Level 1....................................9

Level 2...................................19

Level 3...................................31

Level 4A.................................42

Level 4B.................................50

Level 5A.................................58

Level 5B.................................72

Level 6...................................88

Level 7..................................105

Summer Brainiac Award! 128

Outside Quests..........................129

Answer Key.............................134

Summer Brain Quest Reading List..........145

Summer Brain Quest Mini Deck............154

Your Quest

Your quest is to sticker as many paths on the map as possible and reach the final destination by the end of summer to become an official Summer Brainiac.

Basic Components

Summer progress map

100+ pages of exercises

100+ quest stickers

8 Outside Quests

8 Outside Quest stickers

Over 40 achievement stickers

Summer Brainiac Award

100% sticker

Setup

Detach the map and place it on a flat surface.

Begin at **START** on your map.

How to Play

To advance along a path, you must complete a quest exercise with the matching color and symbol. For example:

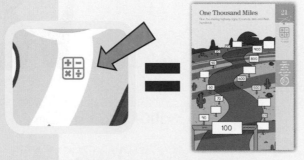

Math exercise from the orange level (Level 2)

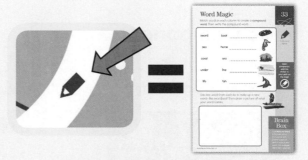

English language arts exercise from the red level (Level 3)

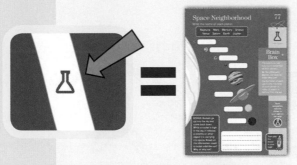

Science exercise from the blue level (Level 5B)

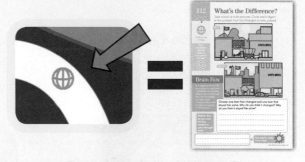

Social studies exercise from the green level (Level 7)

If you complete the challenge, you earn a matching quest sticker.

Place the quest sticker on the path to continue on your journey.

At the end of each leg of your journey, you earn an achievement sticker.

Apply it to the map and move on to the next level!

Forks in Your Path

When you reach a fork in your path, you can choose which direction to take. However, each level must be completed in its entirety. For example, you cannot lay two quest stickers down on Level 4A and then switch to Level 4B.

If you complete one level, you can return to the fork in the path and complete the other level.

Outside Quests

Throughout the map, you will encounter paths that lead to Outside Quests.

To advance along those paths, you must complete one of the Outside Quests.

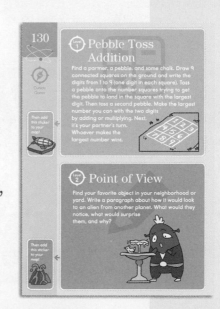

If you complete an Outside Quest, you earn an Outside Quest sticker and advance toward 100% completion!

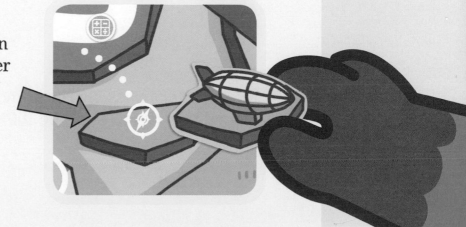

Bonuses

If you complete a bonus question, you earn an achievement sticker.

> **BONUS: Write a sentence with at least two adjectives about a propeller plane.**

Now add this sticker to your map!

Subject Completion

If you complete all of the quest exercises in a subject (math, English language arts, science, or social studies), you earn an achievement sticker.

> **CONGRATULATIONS!** You completed all of your science quests! You earned:

Summer Brain Quest Completion Sticker and Award

If you complete your quest, you earn a Summer Brain Quest completion sticker and award!

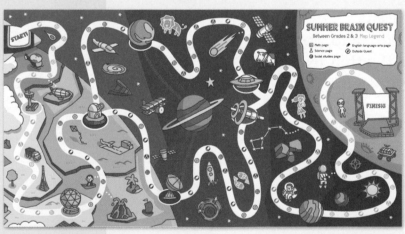

100% Sticker

Sticker *every* possible route and finish *all* the Outside Quests to earn the 100% sticker!

Level
1

Prefixes and Suffixes

3, 2, 1 . . . Blast Off!

Complete each word using a prefix or a suffix.

Upon completion, add this sticker to your path on the map!

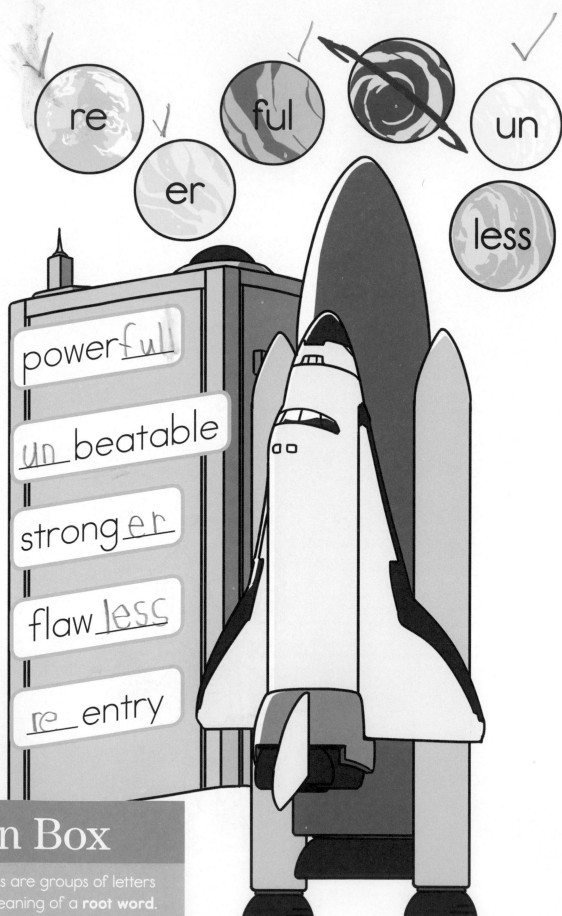

re

er

ful

un

less

powerful

un beatable

stronger

flaw less

re entry

Brain Box

Prefixes and suffixes are groups of letters that change the meaning of a **root word**. A **prefix** appears at the beginning of a word. A **suffix** appears at the end.

How Much Longer?

Write these measurements of time in order from shortest to longest.

✓ week   ✓ day   ✓ minute   year   ✓ second

✓ month   century   ✓ hour   decade

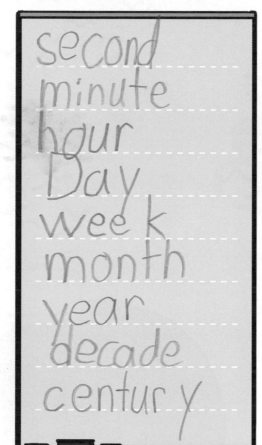

second
minute
hour
Day
week
month
year
decade
century

Write the unit of time from above that best describes how long each action would take.

Press a button to launch a spaceship.

Observe stars in summer, fall, winter, and spring.

Cloud Counting

Is the number of birds in each cloud an even or odd amount? Circle each pair of birds. Then write the number of birds in each cloud and whether it is even or odd.

Even and Odd

Upon completion, add this sticker to your path on the map!

16 even

13 odd

25 odd

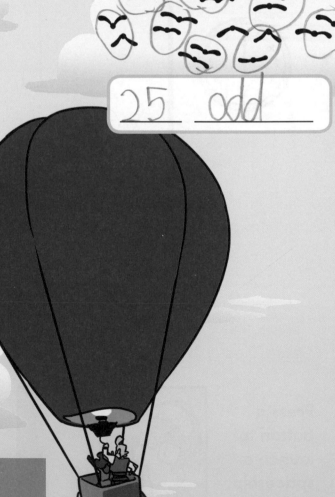

22 even

Brain Box

An **even** number is a whole number that ends in **0**, **2**, **4**, **6**, or **8**. An **even number** of objects makes pairs.

An **odd** number is a whole number that ends in **1**, **3**, **5**, **7**, or **9**. An **odd number** of objects does not make pairs.

Swift or Slow Science

Write whether each event happens **suddenly** or **gradually**.

erosion

_____

volcanic ash cloud

_____

Earth Events

earthquake

_____

glacier formation

_____

Upon completion, add this sticker to your path on the map!

BONUS: If a small comet hit the earth, would it cause changes suddenly or over longer periods of time? What type of change could it cause?

_____

_____

_____

_____

Now add this sticker to your map!

Brain Box

Global and regional changes in the environment can be **sudden** (volcanic eruptions), **gradual** (ice ages), or **long-term** (the movement of the earth's crust).

Families in the Sky

Add or subtract to complete the equations
in each fact family.

Addition and
Subtraction

$6 + 9 = 15$ $9 + 6 = 15$

$15 - 9 = 6$ $15 - 6 = 6$

$8 + 7 = 15$ $7 + 8 = 15$

$15 - 8 = 7$ $15 - 7 = 8$

Brain Box

A **fact family** is a set of related equations,
each of which uses the same three numbers
through addition and subtraction.

___8___ + 6 = 14   6 + 8 = __14__

__14__ – 6 = 8   14 – 8 = __6___

7 + ____ = 12   5 + ____ = 12

12 – 5 = ____   ____ – 7 = 5

Where in the World?

Fill in the missing commas in each sentence.

The desert-dwelling Arzauns are comet jumpers which means they travel by comet.

To catch a ride on a comet they use a strong lasso.

They wait for comets to swing by then loop their rope around them and hop on!

Arzauns call comets "dirty snowballs" because they contain dust ice gases and more.

Comets travel fast like spaceships but they are hard to steer.

However unlike a spaceship you can't just stop a comet anywhere you want.

Brain Box

A **comma** is used to indicate a pause in a sentence and to separate words in a list of three or more things.

So Arzauns dont always know where theyll wind up!

Fortunately, Arzauns dont mind.

Theyre always up for exploring someone elses world.

Thats because Arzauns have a superpower: Wherever they go, they can always make friends.

So wherever they land, theyre glad to be there!

Commas, Apostrophes, and Contractions

Upon completion, add these stickers to your path on the map!

Brain Box

A **contraction** is two words that are joined together. When the two words are joined, some of the letters in the second word are replaced by an **apostrophe**. For example, **I am** becomes **I'm.** Singular and plural nouns are also made possessive by adding an **apostrophe.** For example, Halley**'s** comet or the Arzauns**'** lassos.

Scientific Observation

18

What in the World?

Answer each question using one of the words from the box.

sight	stick	thermometer
touch	scale	notebook

Which is the best tool to find out the weight of a meteorite?

Which is the best tool to find out how hot a meteorite is?

Which is the best sense to use to find out the color of a meteorite?

Which is the best tool to record what you see, touch, and smell?

Which is the best tool to find out if a meteorite is soft or hard without touching it with your hand?

Which is the best sense to use to find out whether a meteorite is rough or smooth?

Upon completion, add this sticker to your path on the map!

Brain Box

Observation is the act of studying and gathering information about something. An observation can include the color, texture, hardness, and flexibility of a living or nonliving object. Observation is the basis of all science!

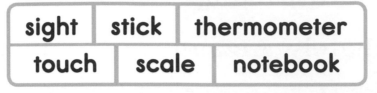

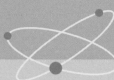

Level 1 complete!

Add this achievement sticker to your path…

…and move on to

Level 2!

Double Desert

Write the plural form of each word. Then circle the plural form in the word search. Words go across and down.

star _____   tale _____

dune _____   grass _____

hat _____   lamp _____

bush _____   fox _____

camel _____   mirage _____

```
D U N E S O I L C W
V Z H A T S B A A Y
P F S Z J N H M M B
G R A S S E S P E S
F B Q P E J M S L T
E L N B U S H E S A
T A L E S I H W G R
P C Q M I R A G E S
B O X I B F O X E S
```

Brain Box

Plural means more than one. Add an **s** to make most nouns plural. Add an **es** if the noun ends in **sh**, **ch**, **tch**, **s**, or **x**.

One Thousand Miles

To fill in the missing highway signs, count by tens on one side and hundreds on the other.

Upon completion, add this sticker to your path on the map!

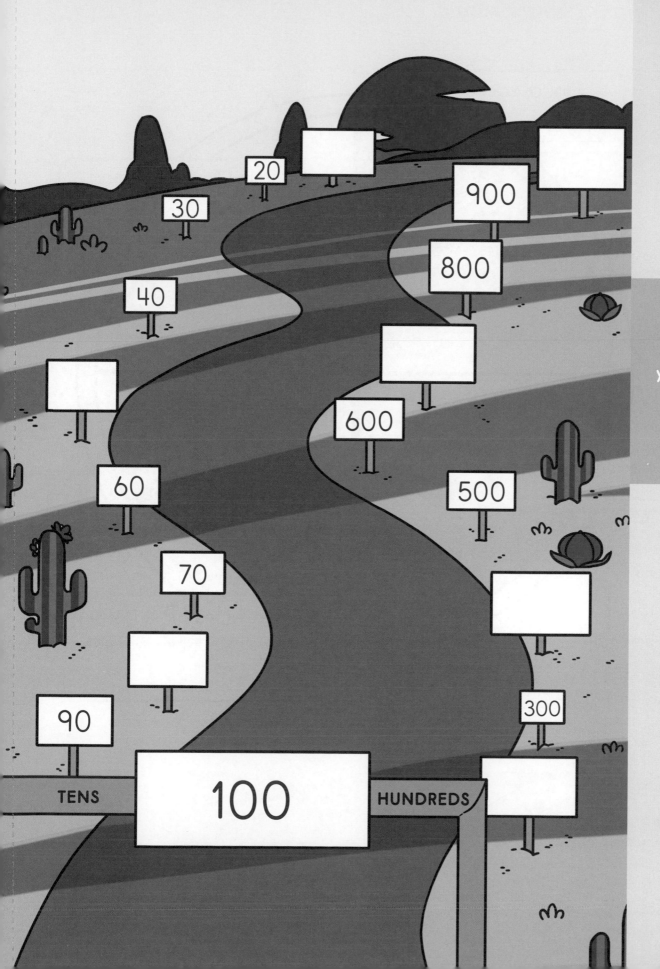

TENS

HUNDREDS

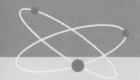

Water Cycle

Where's the Water?

Label the events in the water cycle below as **condensation**, **precipitation**, **collection**, or **evaporation**.

Clouds rain down.

_____

Rain fills up the pond.

_____

Evaporated water forms clouds in the sky.

_____

Water from the oasis turns from liquid into gas.

_____

Upon completion, add this sticker to your path on the map!

Brain Box

Over 70 percent of the earth's surface is covered in water! This water is constantly moving. The **water cycle** shows how it moves over the earth, under the earth, and through the atmosphere.

The Long and Short of It

Write each long and short vowel word from the box on the correct basket.

sand	bead
snake	skin
tune	laugh
dance	song
bite	blue

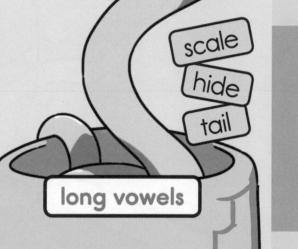

Long and Short Vowels

Upon completion, add this sticker to your path on the map!

drum
red
fast

scale
hide
tail

short vowels

long vowels

_____

_____

_____

_____

_____

_____

_____

_____

Brain Box

A long vowel sounds like the letter, for example, like the **a** in **snake**. Short vowels sound different from the letter, for example, like the **a** in **bat**.

Read the Clues

Answer each question using the
information provided on the map.

Map Skills

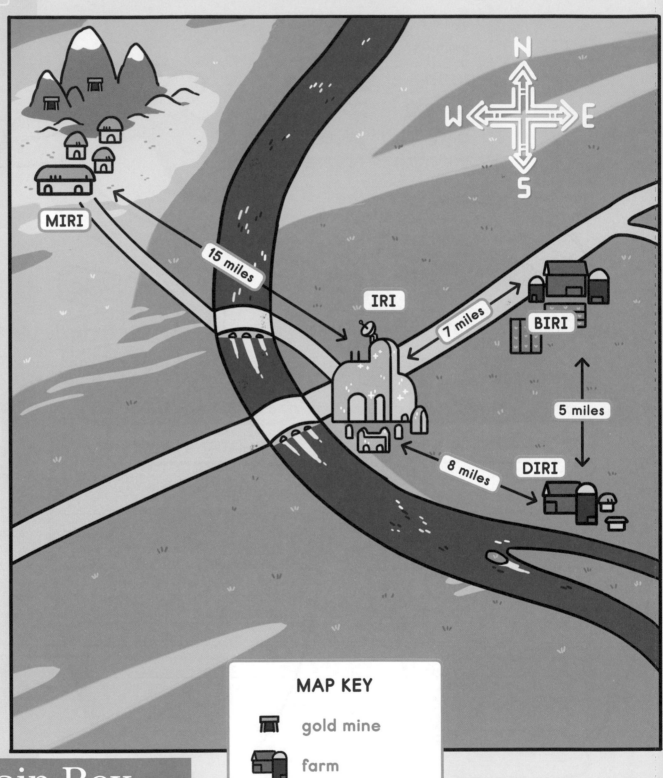

MIRI

15 miles

IRI

7 miles

BIRI

5 miles

8 miles

DIRI

MAP KEY

 gold mine

 farm

 government
building

palace

Brain Box

A **map** is a picture or chart of
something, like the earth's surface.

A **compass rose** shows the four
directions: **N**orth, **S**outh, **E**ast, **W**est.

A **key** or **legend** explains the small
pictures or symbols on the map.

Which city is farther north: Biri or Diri?

_____

Which city is farthest west?

_____

How many cities are NOT on a river?

_____

Which city is closer to Iri: Biri or Diri?

_____

Where might people in Iri get most of their food?

_____

What are two possible reasons why Iri is the biggest city on the map?

_____

_____

_____

Why might someone choose to live in Miri, when it is so far away from water?

_____

What might people in Miri need from people in Iri, Biri, and Diri?

_____

What might people in Iri, Biri, and Diri want from Miri?

_____

Map Skills

Upon completion, add these stickers to your path on the map!

BONUS: You're in Miri, and bandits are robbing the gold mine! How many miles do you need to travel to get help and which city do you go to?

Now add this sticker to your map!

26

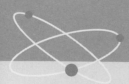

Place Value

Radio Waves

Broadcast each number by writing each digit in the correct place on the chart.

	Hundreds	Tens	Ones
157	1	5	7
200			
823			
68			
375			
240			

Brain Box

You can use **place value** to figure out how much numerals are worth. If you see three numerals, you know that the number is made up of hundreds, tens, and ones. In **624**, there are **6** hundreds, **2** tens, and **4** ones.

Hundreds	Tens	Ones
6	2	4

Place Value

Hundreds	Tens	Ones	
3	0	0	300
7	6	6	
4	0	5	
	7	9	
1	9	0	

Upon completion, add these stickers to your path on the map!

BONUS: The tower broadcasts a number that has 1 in the tens place, 4 in the ones place, and 9 in the hundreds place. What number is it?

Now add this sticker to your map!

Risky Riddles

Read the story from Greek mythology. Then answer each question.

Once upon a time, far out in the sandy plateau of Giza, there lived a Sphinx, a giant beast with the head of a woman and the body of a lion. All day long, she would wag her tail and wait for travelers to come by. Whenever someone finally did dare to pass, the Sphinx always said, "You cannot pass unless you answer my riddle! What creature first walks on four legs, then on two legs, and ends by walking on three legs?" If the explorer did not answer correctly, the hungry Sphinx would make the traveler into her lunch!

One day, a king named Oedipus wandered into the Sphinx's desert home during a long hike. When the Sphinx asked the riddle, Oedipus thought and thought. He thought of all the strange creatures he'd ever seen during his reign as king and during his travels all over the world. He thought for so long that he had to lean on his walking stick to stay standing. That was it! A baby crawls on hands and knees at the beginning of their life. That's like having four legs. An older person walks on two legs. And sometimes an old person uses a cane—a third leg! "Human beings!" Oedipus said. With that, he beat the Sphinx and was able to pass by.

What are some characteristics of the Sphinx?

_____

_____

_____

What is the central message in this story? (Include important characters and events from the text.)

_____

_____

What happens if a traveler can't answer the Sphinx's question?

_____

Does the story tell you the answer to the Sphinx's question? If yes, who answers the riddle correctly?

_____

Do you think that is a good ending to the story? Why or why not?

_____

_____

_____

What might happen in a sequel to this story?

_____

_____

_____

Reading Comprehension

Upon completion, add these stickers to your path on the map!

Digital Domes

Write each number with a 5 in the hundreds place in the **red** dome. Write each number with a 7 in the ones place in the **blue** dome. Write each number with a 3 in the tens place in the **green** dome. (HINT: Numbers can be in more than one dome.)

Upon completion, add this sticker to your path on the map!

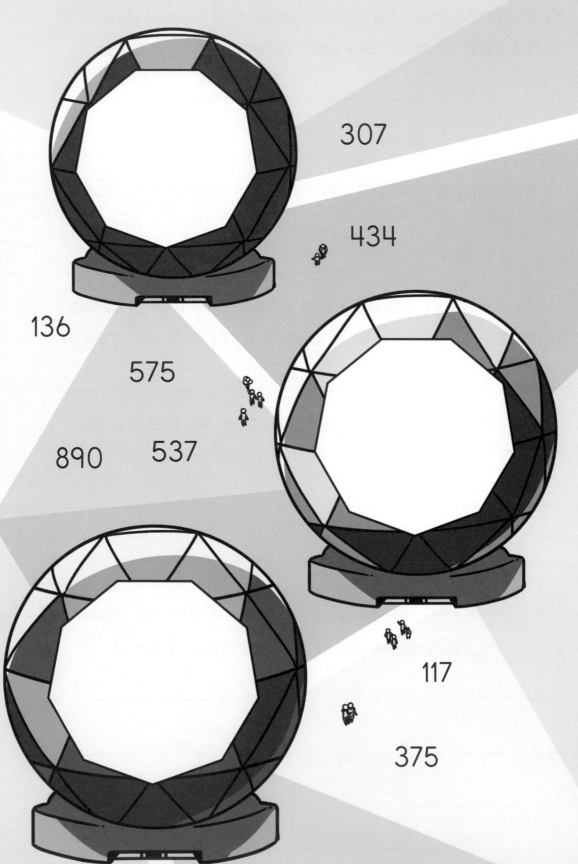

307

434

136

575

890   537

117

375

Level 2 complete!

Add this achievement sticker
to your path...

...and move on to

Level
3!

Sky Woman's Power

Many native people call North America **Turtle Island**. Number each passage of the story in the correct sequence to learn why.

Native American Folklore

Upon completion, add this sticker to your path on the map!

But Sky Woman had a special power. If she had even a small bit of earth, she could make more earth. Enough for everyone to live on.

Sky Woman placed the earth on a turtle's back. Then she used her powers to make more and more land—until the tiny bit of earth grew into what is now called North America!

One by one, each animal dove, but none of them reached the bottom. Finally, only the tiny muskrat was left.

However, there was no earth to be found! So Sky Woman asked all the animals to dive to the bottom of the ocean and bring some earth back up to the surface.

Once, a great flood covered the world. Sky Woman came down to Earth, but there was no place for her to rest—just miles and miles of water, all over.

The muskrat was gone all day and all night. But in the morning, his furry whiskers broke the surface of the water, and after a deep breath, he offered his paw filled with a tiny bit of earth!

Now add this sticker to your map!

BONUS: How does Sky Woman remake the world?

_____

_____

_____

Word Magic

Match words in each column to create a **compound word**. Then write the compound word.

Compound Words

sword	boat	_____
sea	horse	_____
coast	sea	_____
under	line	_____
life	fish	_____

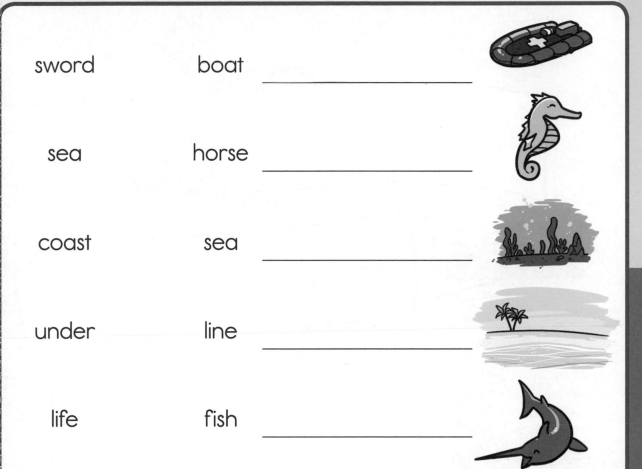

Upon completion, add this sticker to your path on the map!

Use one word from each list to make up a new word—like swordboat! Then draw a picture of what your word names.

Brain Box

A **compound word** is formed when two words are joined together and create a new word. For example, star + fish = starfish!

Hundreds of Leagues Under the Sea

Write the **standard form** of the number that is described on each banner.

Place Value

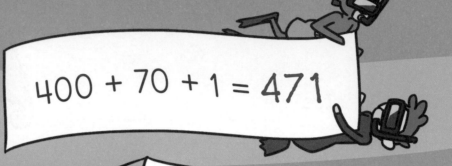

$$400 + 70 + 1 = 471$$

eight hundred forty-six =

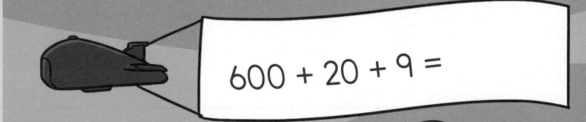

$$600 + 20 + 9 =$$

six hundred ninety-three =

four hundred eighty =

Brain Box

There are different ways you can write a number. For example:

Standard form = **246**

Expanded form = **200 + 40 + 6**

Written form = **two hundred forty-six**

five hundred six =

one hundred seventeen =

500 + 60 + 2 =

Upon
completion,
add these
stickers to
your path on
the map!

300 + 90 + 9 =

BONUS: Your boat is about to dock. It is only **253** feet from the shore. Write the expanded form of the distance.

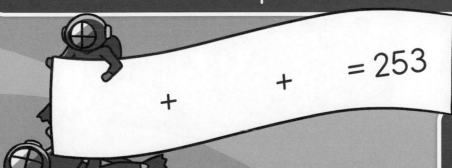

_____ + _____ + _____ = 253

Now add this
sticker to
your map!

Point of View

Land or Sea

Read the articles and answer each question with a complete sentence.

Landlubber News

CANNONBALL CONTEST CANCELED

Today's cannonball contest was canceled when, for no reason, a school of angry fish began to bite the contestants. "This is awful!" one parent fumed.

"Those fish don't belong there! This is our beach!" another said. "Now how are we going to decide who gets to go on the prize boat ride?"

THE SEA TIMES

ATTACK OF THE AIR-BREATHERS

Our sea is under attack! Early this morning, without warning, several air-breathers plunged into the sea and created giant thrashing waves. With quick thinking, all of our gilled cousins were able to band together to chase them away. But who knows when they'll be back again? An anti-air-breather plan must be created.

Who wrote each article?

_____

_____

Why do you think the fish thought they were being attacked?

_____

_____

Did the fish have a reason to be upset at the people? Why or why not?

_____

_____

Why were the people upset?

_____

_____

If you were a fish, would you be upset if a person cannonballed into your world? Why or why not?

_____

_____

Would you get rid of fish at beaches if you could? Why or why not?

_____

_____

How do the different points of view affect the articles?

_____

_____

Upon completion, add these stickers to your path on the map!

BONUS: Rewrite the events from the perspective of a kite flying above the cannonball contest.

_____

_____

_____

_____

Now add this sticker to your map!

Diversity and
Environment

So Many Stinkbugs

Look at the different stinkbugs. Then answer each
question and explain your answers.

A.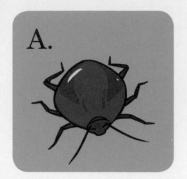

B.

C.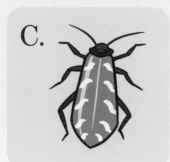

Upon
completion,
add this
sticker to
your path on
the map!

Which bug would be the hardest to see on a black roof?

_____

_____

Which bug would be the hardest to see on a red rose?

_____

_____

Which bug would have the easiest time getting out of a tight space?

_____

_____

Which bug would have the easiest time climbing something tall?

_____

_____

Why might a stinkbug release a stinky smell?

_____

_____

Brain Box

A **conclusion** is a judgment or decision made after a
period of research and thought. To reach a conclusion, use
reason and logic to think about the information available.

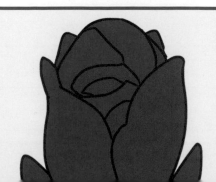

Starry Souvenirs

You have the exact amount of money for each souvenir.
Write the amount you have paid for each souvenir.

Adding Money

Upon completion, add this sticker to your path on the map!

92¢

Brain Box

penny = 1¢

nickel = 5¢

dime = 10¢

quarter = 25¢

dollar bill = $1

People and Environment

Upon completion, add this sticker to your path on the map!

Changing Your World

Draw a line to match each situation with an action that would have a positive impact on the environment.

If you have an empty bottle, you could

If you wanted to get some fresh air inside, you could

If you wanted to see the stars at night, you could

If you were tired of sitting in traffic, you could

If you cut down a tree, you could

ride a bike.

plant another one.

recycle it.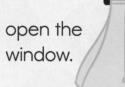

open the window.

turn off the outdoor lights.

Brain Box

People can **impact** or affect the environment in negative and positive ways. Some examples of negative human impact include abusing water and land resources and polluting the water, air, or ground. Some examples of positive human impact include protecting endangered animals, recycling, and conserving water.

What else could a person change in his or her daily life that would help the environment?

_____

_____

Is there any part of the environment you wouldn't like to change? Why do you like it just the way it is?

_____

_____

Level 3 complete!

Add this achievement sticker to your path...

...and move on to

Level 4A

on page 42!

...or move on to

Level 4B

on page 50!

Comparing
Numbers

START
LEVEL
4A
HERE!

Space Adventure Camp

Compare the number of seconds each camper
took to build a robot in a low-gravity simulator.
Write **<**, **=**, or **>** in each circle.

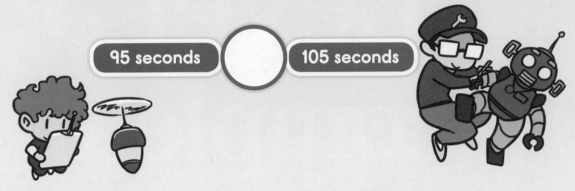

95 seconds 〇 105 seconds

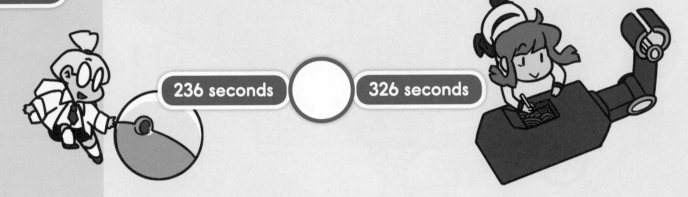

236 seconds 〇 326 seconds

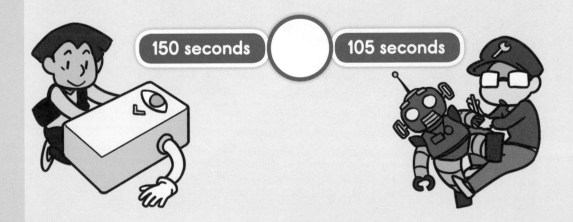

150 seconds 〇 105 seconds

Brain Box

< means **less than.**
> means **greater than.**

Example: **2 < 6**
The less than sign tells us
that **2** is less than **6**.

Example: **7 > 5**
The greater than sign tells
us that **7** is greater than **5**.

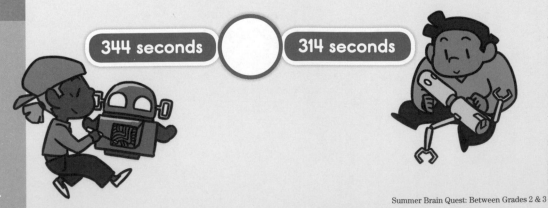

344 seconds 〇 314 seconds

Compare the number of seconds each camper took to complete the rope challenge. Write **<**, **=**, or **>** in each circle.

681 seconds ◯ 618 seconds

423 seconds ◯ 423 seconds

707 seconds ◯ 710 seconds

787 seconds ◯ 878 seconds

Comparing Numbers

Upon completion, add these stickers to your path on the map!

Engineering
Design

What Tools Do Astronauts Use?

Write which tool would best solve each problem.

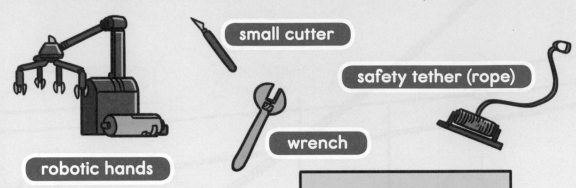

small cutter

safety tether (rope)

wrench

robotic hands

Your dinner is wrapped in plastic.

_____

Brain Box

A **tool** is an object that we create to solve a problem.

Because there is no gravity, you can float away from the spaceship while repairing its shield.

_____

The motion from liftoff loosened a bolt, and it has wiggled out of place.

_____

A piece of space junk got stuck in a crack beyond where you can reach.

_____

BONUS: You must complete a secret mission. Circle which aircraft you would choose.

Now add this sticker to your map!

Model Measures

Get a ruler, or cut out the ruler on page 144. Use it to measure each rocket to the nearest inch and then the nearest centimeter.

Measurement

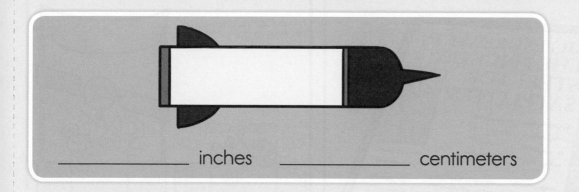

_____ inches   _____ centimeters

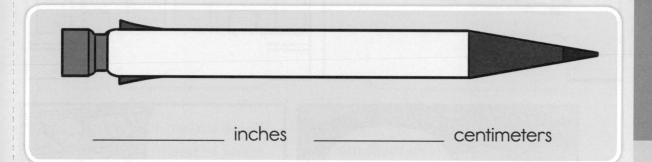

_____ inches   _____ centimeters

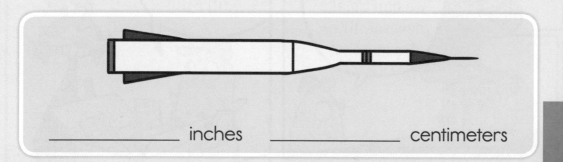

_____ inches   _____ centimeters

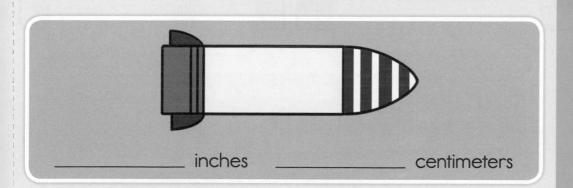

_____ inches   _____ centimeters

Brain Box

Inches, feet, yards, and miles are the standard units of measurement for length in the United States. Centimeters, meters, and kilometers are the units of length in the metric system, which is used outside the United States and by scientists throughout the world.

Economics

Upon completion, add this sticker to your path on the map!

Satellite Sale!

Predict whether each event will lead to lower or higher prices of satellites. Write "lower prices" or "higher prices" next to each event.

Brain Box

Prices of goods usually go up when there's more **demand**. That means there is less of something than people want. For example, the price of bathing suits may go up during the summer because the demand increases.

Prices usually go down when there's plenty of **supply**. That means there is more of a good than people want to buy. For example, the price of footballs may go down if there are more footballs than football players.

BONUS: If someone invented a new satellite that's better than the old ones, would you expect the price of the old ones to go up or down?

_____ → Now add this sticker to your map!

Timely Takeoffs

Draw hands on each clock to show each launch time.

Telling Time

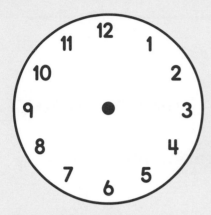

The space plane takes off
at 2:00 p.m.

The spacecraft takes off
at 6:55 a.m.

Upon completion, add this sticker to your path on the map!

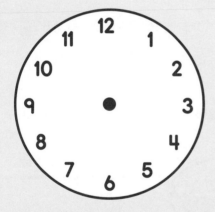

The spaceship takes off
at 11:05 a.m.

The rocket takes off
at 12:25 p.m.

Brain Box

An analog clock has three parts:

- A clock face
- A little hand that points to the hour
- A big hand that points to the minute

TICKETS

Scenic trip!

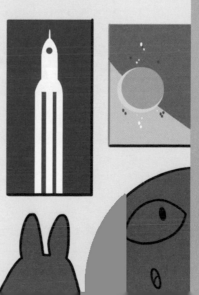

Which Is Worse?

Each pair of words below has similar meanings. Circle the more negative descriptive word to complete each sentence.

"I'm **cold** **freezing**," Zim complained.

"Well, it's not my fault we're lost," Bim **replied** **snapped**.

The two of them were **unhappy** **miserable** about being lost in space.

There had been **nothing** **not much** for them to eat for days.

Just when they thought they might be **starving** **hungry**, the Space Guard found them and towed them home.

"We never want to get **delayed** **stuck** like that again," they agreed.

Upon completion, add this sticker to your path on the map!

BONUS: Write two adjectives that have similar meanings to describe an airplane.

_____

_____

Now add this sticker to your map!

Brain Box

Some words mean almost the same thing but have different shades of meaning. The difference between them is called **nuance**.

Level 4A complete!

Add this achievement sticker to your path…

…AND GO ON AN OUTSIDE QUEST AND MOVE ON TO LEVEL 5B ON PAGE 72!

…or move on to

Level 5A

on page 58!

Fill in the Blanks

Complete the story with adjectives. Then draw a creature that matches your story.

Descriptive
Words

START
LEVEL
4B
HERE!

At first, Esmeralda thought the loud thumping she heard was only a meteor shower. But it didn't stop all night. The next morning, she found a _____ creature with _____ eyes and _____ scales outside her ship.

"I'm Argo," the creature said. "May I borrow your spaceship?"

"No way!" Esmeralda said.

Argo looked very _____. "Then how am I going to get home?" he asked.

"I'll fly you home. I've never seen a creature like you before, and I'm curious where you came from."

"That would be _____!" Argo said.

Together they flew through space to Argo's planet. When they arrived, Esmeralda was amazed by the _____ sky filled with _____.

Brain Box

An **adjective** is a word that describes a person, place, or thing. It can tell us how something looks, feels, tastes, smells, or sounds.

Descriptive
Words

clouds twinkling over a _____ valley.
And everywhere she looked, there were creatures
just like Argo—they had _____ hands and
a very _____ head. They were all flying
_____ propeller planes, like the ones used
on Earth over fifty years ago.

"What do you think?" Argo asked.

"Wow," Esmeralda said. "It's the most _____
world I've ever seen!"

Upon
completion,
add these
stickers to
your path on
the map!

BONUS: Write a sentence with at least
two adjectives about a propeller plane.

_____

_____

Now add this
sticker to your
map!

Past, Present, and Future

Number each picture of the story in the correct sequence to learn how Johnny Appleseed made a difference in history. Then answer the question.

He was so excited about apples that he shared his fruit with others and showed them how to plant a tree.

Then, he watered the small shoot.

Upon completion, add this sticker to your path on the map!

When the shoot finally grew into a tree, he tried his first apple—it was delicious!

Johnny was learning how to plant apple trees. First, he planted the seed.

Soon he became known as Johnny Appleseed, and all over the country, many new apple orchards could be seen.

How did Johnny Appleseed impact other people's lives?

_____

_____

_____

Brain Box

A **cause** tells why something happens. An **effect** is what happens.

Spy Strategy

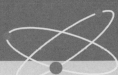

An alien spy is trying to trick you into opening the door to your spaceship. The problem is, he doesn't know English very well. Choose the correct plural noun to complete each sentence.

There's a space beast here with many **tooth** **teeth** **tooths** ! Let me in! He's just a few **foots** **feet** **foot** away from the door.

Are there **children** **childrens** **childs** on board? I have lots of candy to share! Even enough for all the **person** **people** **persons** on your ship.

Hurry up and open the door, before the space **wolf** **wolfs** **wolves** get here!

Brain Box

Some words don't follow the rules for making plurals. These are called **irregular plurals**. Instead of adding an **s** or **es** at the end to make the word plural, you have to change the whole word.

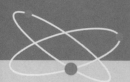

Objects and
Their Parts

Put It Back Together Again

Draw and write how you can disassemble the objects and use the materials to solve each problem.

wood fence

brick wall

wagon

SPACE HALL OF FAME

_____

_____

_____

Climbing stairs

Crossing a valley

_____

_____

_____

BONUS: If you wanted to travel a far distance, what objects around you could you use to build a vehicle?

_____

_____

Now add this sticker to your map!

Nebula Popularity

Space campers vote for their favorite nebula (swirling clouds of gas and dust). Solve each word problem by adding or subtracting.

Addition and Subtraction Within 100

Diamond Ring

23 campers vote for the Diamond Ring nebula and 57 campers vote for Rosette. How many campers in all vote for Diamond Ring and Rosette?

```
  23
+ 57
----
```

Rosette

Owl

How many more campers vote for the Rosette nebula than vote for Diamond Ring?

```
  57
- 23
----
```

Upon completion, add this sticker to your path on the map!

Soccer Ball

Fried Egg

35 campers vote for the Owl nebula, but 33 more vote for Soccer Ball. How many vote for Soccer Ball?

```
  35
+ 33
----
```

Brain Box

Word problems have phrases that tell you what operation you need to do to solve the problem.

Running Chicken

60 campers vote for the Fried Egg nebula and 38 campers vote for Running Chicken. How many fewer campers vote for Running Chicken than for Fried Egg?

```
  60
- 38
----
```

Addition Clue Words:
total number
in all
altogether

Subtraction Clue Words:
how many more/less/ fewer
how many are left
the difference

BONUS: Thirty-six campers vote for the Necklace nebula. Then you and 10 friends also vote for it. How many votes in all would that be?

Necklace

_____ + _____ = _____ people

Now add this sticker to your map!

Space Vacation on Para-Dice

Circle the correct past tense verb to use in each sentence.

Irregular
Past Tense

Upon completion, add this sticker to your path on the map!

Dear Seth,

I **had** **haved** a great vacation! First, my family **sitted** **sat** under the warm pink sun. Then, we **drank** **drinked** sweet momo fruit juice and **ate** **eated** piles of space fries. We also **go** **went** to a festival and **heared** **heard** the Para-Dice singers perform their hit song. Every afternoon, flocks of orange birds **flied** **flew** by. Also, I **keeped** **kept** a beautiful shell from the blue stone beach. I am sad to leave, but I'm excited to see you at space school in September!

Sabrina

Brain Box

A **past-tense verb** tells about something that has already happened. You can add **d** or **ed** to most verbs to make them past tense. However, if the verb is an irregular verb, it doesn't follow the same rules as most regular verbs; you may have to change the whole word.

Level 4B complete!

Add this achievement sticker to your path…

…AND GO ON
AN OUTSIDE QUEST
AND MOVE ON
TO LEVEL 5A
ON PAGE 58!

…or move on to

Level 5B

on page 72!

Math Riddle

Add or subtract.

START
LEVEL
5A
HERE!

$$\begin{array}{r} 58 \\ -\ 49 \\ \hline \end{array}$$

R

$$\begin{array}{r} 27 \\ +\ 27 \\ \hline \end{array}$$

G

$$\begin{array}{r} 56 \\ +\ 29 \\ \hline \end{array}$$

F

$$\begin{array}{r} 45 \\ -\ 19 \\ \hline \end{array}$$

P

$$\begin{array}{r} 35 \\ +\ 26 \\ \hline \end{array}$$

N

$$\begin{array}{r} 96 \\ -\ 61 \\ \hline \end{array}$$

E

$$\begin{array}{r} 82 \\ +\ 15 \\ \hline \end{array}$$

A

$$\begin{array}{r} 34 \\ +\ 37 \\ \hline \end{array}$$

O

$$\begin{array}{r} 60 \\ -\ 32 \\ \hline \end{array}$$

L

$$\begin{array}{r} 74 \\ +\ 16 \\ \hline \end{array}$$

T

$$\begin{array}{r} 84 \\ -\ 48 \\ \hline \end{array}$$

H

Use your answers to decode the riddle.

Addition and
Subtraction
Within 100

Riddle:

Why didn't the astronaut
take a vacation?

Answer:

| ___ | ___ | | ___ | ___ | ___ | ___ | ___ | ___ |
| 36 | 35 | | 85 | 71 | 9 | 54 | 71 | 90 |

| ___ | ___ | | ___ | ___ | ___ | ___ | ___ | ___ |
| 90 | 71 | | 26 | 28 | 97 | 61 | 35 | 90 |

Upon
completion,
add these
stickers to
your path on
the map!

Photosynthesis

Upon completion, add this sticker to your path on the map!

Will It Grow?

Read the passage. Then look at each experiment below and answer each question.

You need to eat food to get energy so you can grow. Likewise, plants also need energy to grow, but most plants are able to *make* their own food! They get energy from sunlight and use it, along with air and water, to create their food, called **glucose**. This process is called **photosynthesis**. Plants have a green substance called **chlorophyll** (pronounced *klor-uh-fill*), which uses the light energy from the sun, carbon dioxide from the air, and water from the soil to make glucose.

What will happen to the plant that has only soil, air, and sun but no water? Explain why.

_____

_____

_____

What will happen to the plant that has only soil, air, and water? Explain why.

_____

_____

_____

Circle the plant that will grow well. Explain why.

_____

_____

_____

Leader of Planet X

What laws would you enact if you were the leader of your own planet? Answer each question.

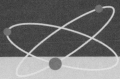

Understanding Laws

What three things would everyone have to do?

_____

_____

_____

What three things would everyone have to stop doing?

_____

_____

_____

How would each law make your planet a better place?

_____

_____

_____

What would you do if someone broke a law?

_____

_____

_____

_____

Upon completion, add this sticker to your path on the map!

BONUS: If a new star was discovered near your planet, and everyone was arguing about whom it belonged to, what law would you pass to solve the problem?

_____

_____

_____

Now add this sticker to your map!

Hundreds of Meteors

Add. Then draw a line through your answers to get through the meteor field. (HINT: You may need to regroup.)

START!

346
+ 152

626
+ 213

133
+ 248

452
+ 288

607
+ 237

465
+ 172

734
+ 188

354
+ 155

Subtract. Then continue the line through your answers to get through the meteor field.
(HINT: You may need to regroup.)

Addition and Subtraction Within 1,000

$$\begin{array}{r} 817 \\ -\ 514 \\ \hline \end{array}$$

$$\begin{array}{r} 955 \\ -\ 332 \\ \hline \end{array}$$

$$\begin{array}{r} 796 \\ -\ 128 \\ \hline \end{array}$$

$$\begin{array}{r} 444 \\ -\ 215 \\ \hline \end{array}$$

$$\begin{array}{r} 739 \\ -\ 374 \\ \hline \end{array}$$

$$\begin{array}{r} 316 \\ -\ 198 \\ \hline \end{array}$$

FINISH!

$$\begin{array}{r} 727 \\ -\ 290 \\ \hline \end{array}$$

$$\begin{array}{r} 830 \\ -\ 188 \\ \hline \end{array}$$

Upon completion, add these stickers to your path on the map!

Growing Up

Read about the life cycles of butterflies, dogs, and robins. Then answer each question.

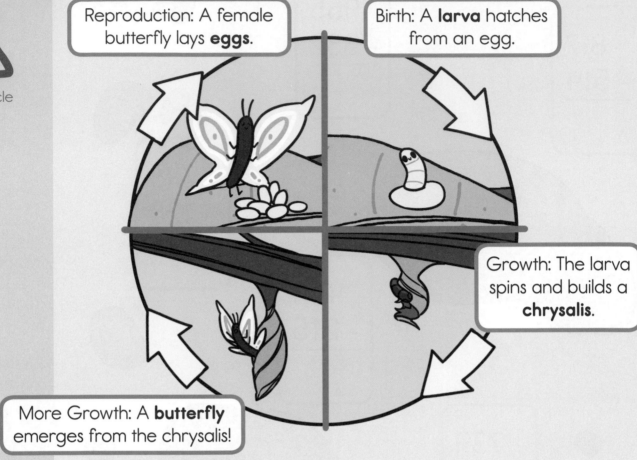

Reproduction: A female butterfly lays **eggs**.

Birth: A **larva** hatches from an egg.

Growth: The larva spins and builds a **chrysalis**.

More Growth: A **butterfly** emerges from the chrysalis!

Reproduction: **Pregnant adult female dogs** carry their puppies for a few months.

Birth: A **litter** of **puppies** is born.

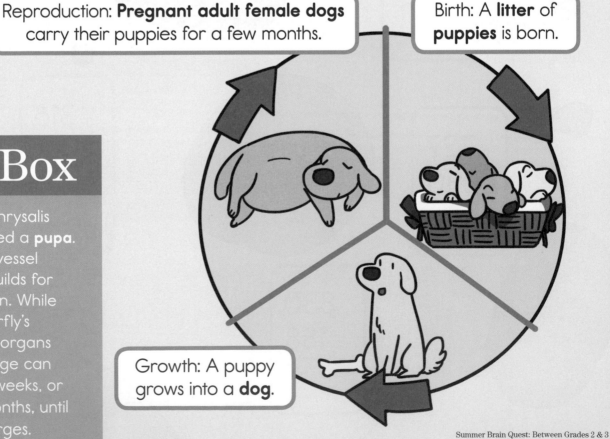

Growth: A puppy grows into a **dog**.

Brain Box

The butterfly's chrysalis can also be called a **pupa**. This is a special vessel that the larva builds for its transformation. While inside, the butterfly's legs, wings, and organs emerge. This stage can last for several weeks, or even several months, until a butterfly emerges.

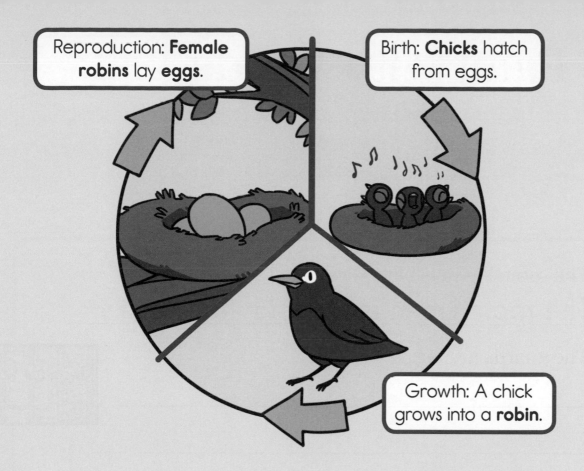

Reproduction: **Female robins** lay **eggs**.

Birth: **Chicks** hatch from eggs.

Growth: A chick grows into a **robin**.

Which of these animals is not born from an egg?

_____

What three stages do all of these life cycles have in common?

_____

_____

What do you notice about the order of these three stages?

_____

_____

_____

Some insects and amphibians go through **metamorphosis**. In butterflies, metamorphosis occurs from the larva through the adult butterfly stages. What happens in this stage that is different from the other animals?

_____

_____

_____

Upon completion, add these stickers to your path on the map!

Paint with Words

Robots have captured you, but you have a chance to escape! The robots don't understand analogies. Rewrite each literal sentence with an analogy in order to tell the rescue team where to find you.

Figurative Language

Upon completion, add this sticker to your path on the map!

~~The room I'm in is blue.~~

The room I'm in is colored like the sky.

The guards are big.

_____

_____

The mountains outside are tall and capped with snow.

_____

_____

We are near a lake full of bubbly orange water.

_____

_____

The weather here is cold.

_____

_____

Brain Box

An **analogy** compares how things are related to each other. For example, "The tiny alien's language was music to the astronaut's ears." The sentence compares a **language** to **music**.

A **simile** is a type of analogy that compares two things using the word **as** or **like**. For example, "The moon was as **bright as a lantern.**" The sentence compares a **moon** to a **lantern**.

Don't Miss the Meteors!

Read each pair of events. One is the **cause** and one is the **effect**. Circle the cause.

Cause and Effect

City parks were full of people excited to see meteors.

Scientists announced a large meteor shower coming soon.

Scientists discovered a galaxy far beyond any they had ever seen.

Scientists built a new, very powerful telescope.

A new icy, round object was slightly too small to be a planet.

Scientists categorized the new satellite as a dwarf planet.

A solar wind blew back the tail of a comet as it shot across the sky.

The outermost layer of the sun expanded into space, causing a solar wind.

Upon completion, add this sticker to your path on the map!

Space Plot

Categorize the satellites by length. Make a tally mark in the correct row of the chart for each satellite. Then write the total number of each satellite.

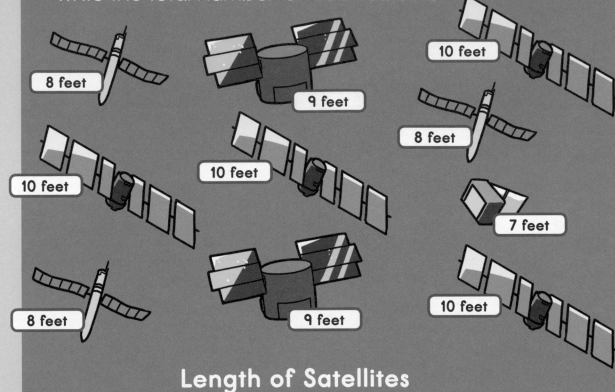

Length of Satellites

Length (feet)	Tally	Total Number
7	/	1
8		
9		
10		

Brain Box

Line plots (also called **dot plots**) can be used to show numerical data. A number line runs along the bottom of the graph. A dot represents how many times that number occurs.

Number of Jet Packs Each Student Owns

2 students own 0 jet packs.

4 students own 1 jet pack.

3 students own 2 or more jet packs.

0   1   2 or more

Create a **dot plot** with the data from your chart.
Draw a dot for each satellite according to length.

Organizing
Data: Dot Plot

Number of Satellites by Length

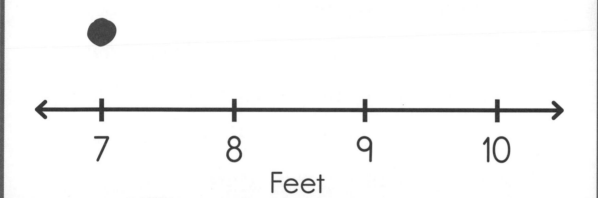

Feet

Upon
completion,
add these
stickers to
your path on
the map!

BONUS: The store sells out of the longest
satellites. How many satellites are left?

_____ satellites

Now add
this sticker
to your
map!

Which Twin?

Circle the correct word to complete each sentence.

Adjectives
versus
Adverbs

Upon
completion,
add this
sticker to
your path on
the map!

Castor and Pollux were twins, but they were **different** **differently**. Castor was **great** **greatly** with horses. He could get any horse to run **quick** **quickly**. Pollux, on the other hand, was incredibly **strong** **strongly**. He could lift a giant boulder **easy** **easily**. Both of them loved being together, and they had all kinds of **interestingly** **interesting** adventures. They traveled to many distant lands, carrying their spears **proud** **proudly** and riding their horses **good** **well**. They also loved their sister, Helen, and together they **brave** **bravely** fought in the Trojan War to rescue her.

Brain Box

An **adverb** describes an adjective, a verb, or another adverb. Adverbs tell **how**, **when**, or **where** an action happens. For example, "The satellite orbited the planet **silently**." The adverb **silently** tells **how** the satellite orbited. Many adverbs end with the suffix **ly**.

Level 5A complete!

Add this achievement sticker to your path…

LEVEL
5B
COMPLETE!

…and move on to

Level 6

on page 88!

Using
Dictionaries

START
LEVEL
5B
HERE!

Out-of-This-World Words

Read the definitions of each word.

behave

verb be·have \bi-'hāv, bē-\
 : to act in an acceptable way: to act properly
 : to act in a particular way

create

verb cre·ate \krē-'āt, 'krē-,\
 : to make or produce (something): to cause
   (something new) to exist
 : to cause (a particular situation) to exist

happy

adjective hap·py \'ha-pē\
 : feeling pleasure and enjoyment because of
   your life, situation, etc.
 : showing or causing feelings of pleasure and
   enjoyment

power

noun pow·er \'pau̇(-ə)r\
 : the ability or right to control people or things
 : political control of a country or area

tell

verb \'tel\
 : to say or write (something) to (someone)
 : to give information to (someone) by speaking
   or writing

Choose a prefix to add to each root word to create a new word. Then write the definition of the new word.

Prefixes

re- pre- **tell**

_____

super- dis- power

_____

un- mis- happy

_____

co- un- create

_____

mis- pre- behave

_____

Upon completion, add these stickers to your path on the map!

Who Made It?

Man-Made
versus Natural

Circle each man-made object.
Cross out each natural object.

planet Earth

stars in sky

landing vehicle

flag

hill in background

an astronaut suit

rover

rocks in foreground

Brain Box

Natural objects are objects found in the environment, and include water, rocks, and trees. Objects created by humans that do not exist naturally in their environments are **man-made**; these include roads, airplanes, and even hamburgers!

Name a man-made object that you might bring to the moon, and explain why you would bring it.

_____

_____

A Capital Idea

Circle the letters that should be capitalized in this tourist brochure.

Capitalization

welcome to the capital city of planet purple!

You're just in time for the plum parade.

rita violet, our mayor, will lead us down plum street.

the purple posse will play music for dancing.

plenty of people will be eating plum pudding–brand ice pops.

kids on floats will throw piles of prizes into the crowds at magenta square.

rick and rhonda lavender will broadcast the show on channel 5, purple tv.

When the parade ends at orchid park, there'll be plenty of delicious eggplant for everyone!

Brain Box

A **common noun** names any person, place, or thing. Common nouns begin with a lowercase letter. For example, **boy**, **country**, **month**.

A **proper noun** is the name of a **specific** person, place, or thing. Proper nouns begin with a capital letter. For example, **David**, **France**, **June**.

Upon completion, add this sticker to your path on the map!

BONUS: Imagine a planet where the only color you see is your favorite color. Name and write about your planet using correct capitalization.

Now add this sticker to your map!

Picture and
Bar Graphs

Space Snacks

Each graph has a different way of
showing the same data. Study the graphs
and answer each question about the
space snacks.

 CRACKERS    COOKIES    CHEESE

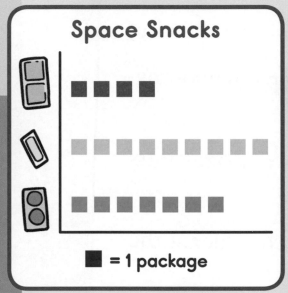

Space Snacks

■ = 1 package

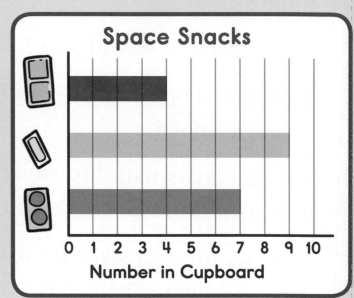

Space Snacks

Number in Cupboard

Which snack is there the most of on board? How many?

_____

How many packages of cookies and crackers are there in all?

_____

How many more packages of cheese snacks than cookies are there?

_____

How many fewer packages of cracker snacks than cookies are there?

_____

What is the total number of packages of snacks?

_____

Space Neighborhood

Write the name of each planet.

Solar System

Neptune   Mars   Mercury   Uranus
Venus   Saturn   Earth   Jupiter

_____

_____

_____

_____

_____

_____

_____

_____

Brain Box

This mnemonic can help you to remember all eight planets:

My **V**ery **E**nergetic **M**artian **J**ust **S**oared **U**nder **N**eptune!

The first letter of each word is the first letter of each planet—in order of closest to farthest from the sun.

Upon completion, add this sticker to your path on the map!

BONUS: A spaceship launches off of Neptune and travels toward the sun. If the spaceship lands on Earth, which planets will it have flown over?

_____
_____
_____

Now add this sticker to your map!

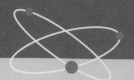

Vowel Sounds

Star System

Write each word from the boxes in the
constellation that has the same vowel sound.
Now add two words of your own.

perch · flew · gray · birch · clue

me · space · speech · coin · moon

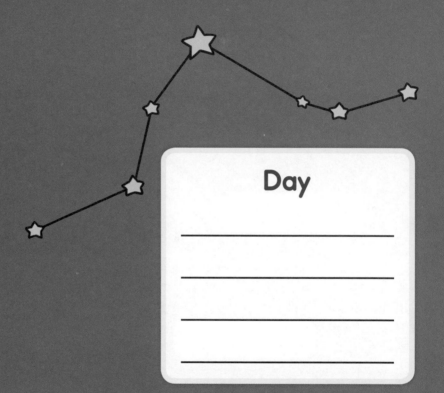

Day

_____

_____

_____

_____

Search

_____

_____

_____

_____

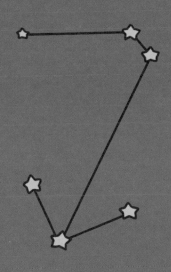

Boy

_____

_____

_____

Vowel Sounds

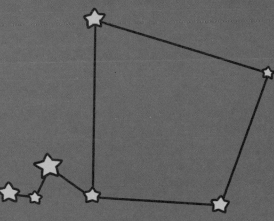

Teach

_____

_____

_____

_____

Upon completion, add these stickers to your path on the map!

Blue

_____

_____

_____

_____

Research

Research It!

Read each research question about the planet of Watoxi, then write where you would look to find the answer.

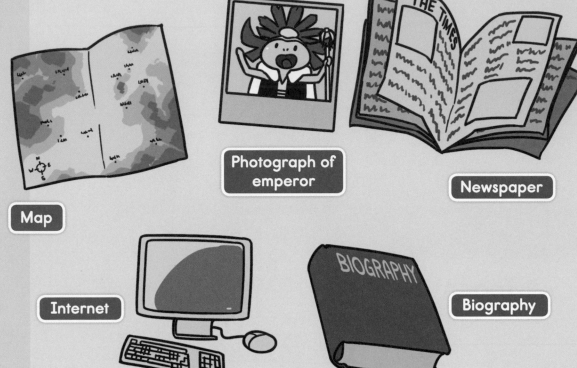

Map

Photograph of emperor

Newspaper

Internet

Biography

What is the life story of Watoxi's most important scientist?

_____

What news articles were published on the first day of the big Watoxi war?

_____

How far is Watoxi's biggest city from the Bubbling Watoxi Sea?

_____

What did the Watoxi emperor wear on the day he took office?

_____

What did the Watoxi people write online about the Spacefruit Festival?

_____

Read the news profile. Then answer each question using complete sentences.

81

Research

Who Is Watoxi's Emperor?

Watoxi's emperor is only seven years old, but he's already made many changes to the planet. A great lover of dogs, he owns twelve of them and has created dog parks all around Watoxi City. He's also installed a roller coaster on the palace grounds, which anyone can ride, free of charge. But he's also capable of serious business. Although his father was never able to work out a treaty with Toboxi, Watoxi's new emperor was able to make an agreement with them—after taking the Toboxi emperor on his roller coaster.

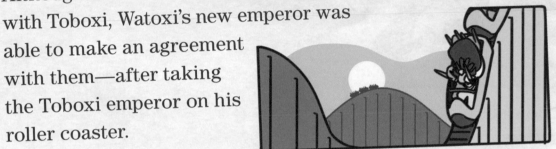

Upon completion, add these stickers to your path on the map!

Does the emperor like dogs? Use two details from the text as evidence for your answer.

_____

_____

What two details from the article are illustrated in the pictures?

_____

_____

Name two key details that you learn from the text that are **not** illustrated in the pictures.

_____

_____

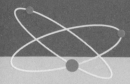

Spacewalks

Solve each word problem by finding the unknown number.

The blue astronaut walked in space for 91 minutes. The next day he spacewalked for another 98 minutes. How many minutes in all were his two walks?

_____ minutes

The purple astronaut spacewalked for 370 minutes. The next day she spacewalked again. If she walked for 480 minutes in total, how many minutes did she walk on the second day?

_____ minutes

Upon completion, add this sticker to your path on the map!

The green astronaut's first spacewalk was 120 minutes long. The second spacewalk was shorter. The total number of minutes for the walks was 200 minutes. How long was his second spacewalk?

_____ minutes

According to the information above, how many minutes shorter was the green astronaut's first spacewalk than the purple astronaut's first spacewalk?

_____ minutes

Secrets in Stars

Write the names on the correct constellation.

Canis Major
(The Great Dog)

Pisces
(The Fish)

Gemini
(The Twins)

Capricornus
(The Sea Goat)

Cygnus
(The Swan)

Leo
(The Lion)

Astronomy

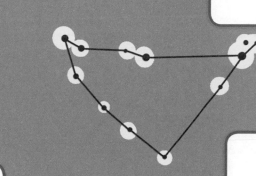

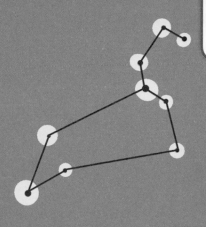

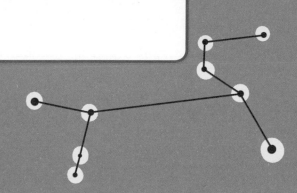

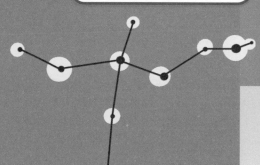

Upon completion, add this sticker to your path on the map!

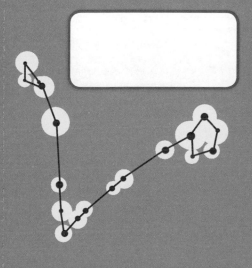

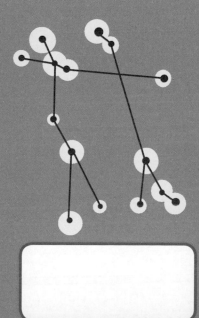

Brain Box

A **constellation** is a group of stars that create a pattern in the sky and can look like a person, object, or animal. Try spotting one of the constellations shown above the next time you're outside at night.

Space Speak ???

This space station has supplies, but you can only get some if you ask the right way. Answer each question according to the instructions.

Would you like freeze-dried ice cream? Write a complete sentence to receive your ice cream.

Complete Sentence Robot

_____

_____

What kind of freeze-dried ice cream would you like? Add an adjective to your sentence to choose your ice cream.

Adjective Robot

_____

_____

How will you eat your freeze-dried ice cream? Write a complete sentence with an adverb to receive your ice cream.

Adverb Robot

_____

_____

Brain Box

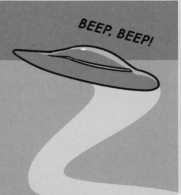

BEEP, BEEP!

An **independent clause** has a subject and a predicate and can stand alone as a **complete sentence**. The subject tells who or what the sentence is about. The predicate tells what the subject is or does.

For example:

The flying saucer	flew around the planet.
subject	**predicate**

A **compound sentence** has two or more independent clauses.

For example:

The flying saucer flew	, and	it blew dust in the air.
independent clause	**comma and conjunction**	**independent clause**

Do you want more supplies? Write a different version of your previous sentence to receive more.

Mix-It-Up Robot

Complete and Compound Sentences

Which two supplies would you like? Write a sentence with two subjects to get two supplies.

Subject Robot

What two things would you like to do with your supplies? Write a sentence with two predicates to get two supplies.

Predicate Robot

Upon completion, add these stickers to your path on the map!

What are two reasons why I should give you these supplies? Write a compound sentence with two reasons to get two supplies.

Compound Sentence Robot

BONUS: Write two complete sentences describing the Pisces constellation. Then combine the sentences into a compound sentence.

Now add this sticker to your map!

Flying Saucer Food

Solve each word problem by filling in the missing numbers in each step.

Theo made 12 saucy sandwiches. Then he made 9 more. His family ate 14 of them. How many sandwiches are left?

STEP 1: 12 + 9 = ☐

STEP 2: ☐ – 14 = ☐ **sandwiches**

Abby had 60 minutes before she had to leave the house. She prepared squash saucers for 20 minutes. Then she baked them for 32 minutes. How much time was left before she had to leave?

STEP 1: 20 + 32 = ☐

STEP 2: 60 – ☐ = ☐ **minutes**

Bea saved $23. She received $25 more for her birthday. Then she spent $30 on winged whoopie pies for her party. How much money did she have left?

STEP 1: $23 + $25 = $☐

STEP 2: $☐ – $30 = $☐

Tina bought 18 chocolate rocket pops and 7 vanilla rocket pops. On her way home, 9 rocket pops melted. How many rocket pops did Tina have left?

STEP 1: 18 + 7 = ☐

STEP 2: ☐ – 9 = ☐ **rocket pops**

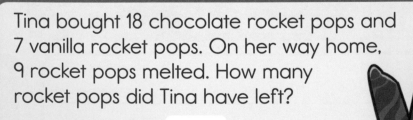

Level 5B complete!

Add this achievement sticker
to your path…

LEVEL
5A
COMPLETE!

…and move on to

Level 6

on page 88!

Artistic Aliens

Write each noun on the correct easel.

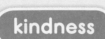

kindness peach globe berry

talent happiness treasure diagram

volcano beauty justice wisdom

START
LEVEL
6
HERE!

Upon
completion,
add this
sticker to
your path on
the map!

Abstract

Concrete

Brain Box

An **abstract noun** names something you can't
touch or see, like ideas, experiences, and feelings.
A **concrete noun** names something you can
touch or see, like any physical object around you.

The Way Through the Stars

You hid treasure in space! Follow the directions to create a map that will lead you back to your treasure.

1. Title your map—you may want to use a code word.
2. Write directions on the compass rose: North, South, East, and West.
3. Fill in the scale: Each square unit is equal to 500 light-years.
4. On the planet with a ring, draw a large lake in the northern hemisphere and a mountain range in the southern hemisphere.
5. Create a symbol to mark where the treasure is hidden. Draw it on the legend.
6. Lastly, draw your symbol on the map where the treasure is hidden!

Maps

Upon completion, add this sticker to your path on the map!

Title

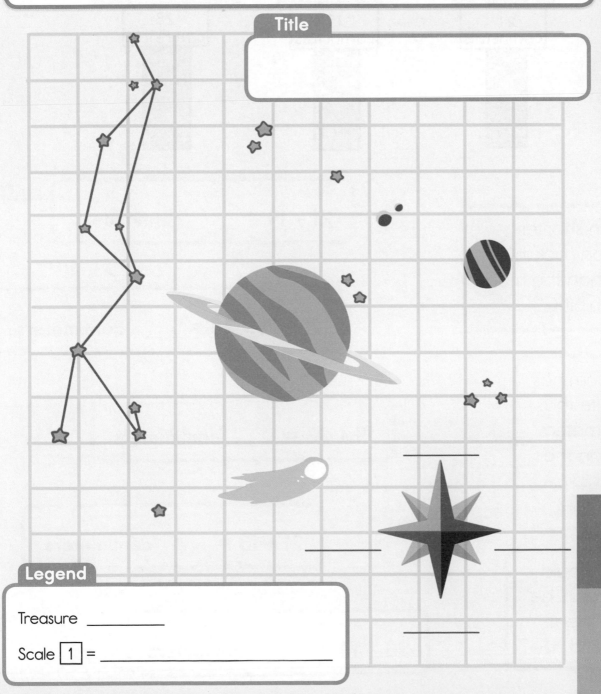

Legend

Treasure _____

Scale 1 = _____

Brain Box

A map's **legend** tells you the meaning of the different symbols on the map.

Word
Problems

Moon Rock Museum

Draw a line to match each word problem to the correct equation. Then write the answer on the line.

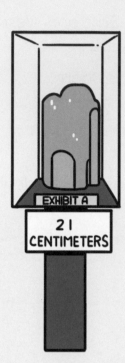

EXHIBIT A

21 CENTIMETERS

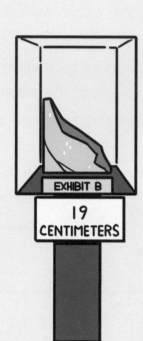

EXHIBIT B

19 CENTIMETERS

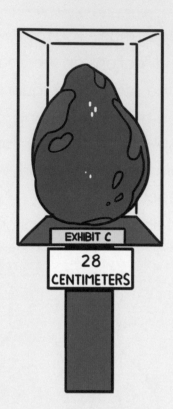

EXHIBIT C

28 CENTIMETERS

How much shorter is the moon rock in Exhibit B than the moon rock in Exhibit C?

21 – 19 = _____ centimeters

21 + 19 + 28 = _____ centimeters

The museum has a meteorite that is 10 centimeters longer than the rock in Exhibit A. How long is it?

19 + 28 = _____ centimeters

21 + 10 = _____ centimeters

How long would all three rocks be if you put them together in a row?

28 – 19 = _____ centimeters

Sightseeing Seeds

Draw the missing step or steps for each pollination process.

Seed Dispersal and Pollination

Upon completion, add this sticker to your path on the map!

The wind carries the seeds of a dandelion.

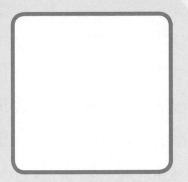

The seeds fall to the ground.

Seeds are inside fruit.

Birds eat the fruit and poop out the seeds.

The seeds fall to the ground.

A bee drinks the nectar of a flower. The flower's pollen from a stamen sticks to the bee.

The bee flies to another flower with the pollen on its hair.

The bee drinks the nectar of the other flower and rubs the pollen on its pistil.

The pollinated flower makes a seed and it falls to the ground.

Brain Box

Animals can move around, but plants cannot. Plants often depend on animals and the wind to help spread their seeds or **pollinate** other plants.

Shape
Attributes

Pretend Planets

You traveled through a wormhole to a galaxy
with unusual planets.

Color each planet with a face that is a triangle **green**.

Color each planet with a face that is a circle **orange**.

Color each planet with a face that is a square **pink**.

Color each planet with a face that is a pentagon **red**.

Color each planet with a face that is a quadrilateral
that is not a square or a rectangle **blue**.

Color each 2-D planet **black**.

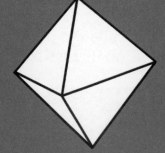

Brain Box

A **2-D** figure has
length and width,
but no thickness.

A **3-D** figure has
length, width, and
thickness. A surface
of a 3-D shape is
called a **face**.

Shape
Attributes

Upon
completion,
add these
stickers to
your path on
the map!

Legends of the Milky Way

Read the legends about the creation of the Milky Way.
Then answer each question.

A Khoisan legend from Africa claims that the sky was once pure black. The story explains that a lonely girl wanted to visit other people, but there was no light to guide her. So she threw embers into the sky to create the Milky Way to light her path.

A Chinese legend says that a goddess created the Milky Way. When her daughter fell in love with a boy, the goddess became angry. She used a pin to draw a silver line between the lovers so that they would be separated forever, and it became the Milky Way.

A Cherokee legend says the Milky Way was created by a dog who wanted some cornmeal. When he stole a bag, he was chased away. The trail of cornmeal that spilled as he ran created the Milky Way.

Brain Box

The **Milky Way** is the galaxy we live in. A **galaxy** is a system of millions or even billions of stars, gas, and dust that are held together by gravity.

Which story has an animal as the main character?

_____

Who are the main female characters in the stories?

_____

_____

Which two stories involve scattering something in the sky?

_____

According to the Khoisan story, how can the Milky Way help people?

_____

_____

In one of the stories, the Milky Way was created by accident. How did this happen?

_____

_____

Choose two legends and write two ways they are alike and two ways they are different.

_____

_____

_____

_____

Write and draw your own legend about how the Milky Way was formed! Include at least one feature to make it similar to the legends and one feature to make it different.

_____

_____

_____

_____

_____

_____

_____

Reading Comprehension

Upon completion, add these stickers to your path on the map!

Economics

Upon completion, add this sticker to your path on the map!

Save or Spend?

Read the passage. Then answer each question.

Ido has been saving up to buy a new jet pack that costs 30 space bucks. Ido's mom gives him 3 space bucks a week for his allowance. Ido can earn 2 more space bucks per week by collecting space rocks around the neighborhood. But he loves buying solar snacks on his way home from school. They cost 1 space buck each.

What does Ido have to choose **not** to have if he wants to buy the jet pack sooner?

_____

If Ido buys a solar snack every week, what is the consequence?

_____

What can Ido do to earn extra space bucks?

_____

_____

What is the fastest way for Ido to save 30 space bucks?

_____

_____

If a jet pack costs the same amount as 30 snacks, which would you rather have, and why?

_____

_____

BONUS: If you wanted to earn money to take a trip to a constellation, what could you do to make and save money?

_____

_____

_____

Now add this sticker to your map!

Past, Present, and Future

Choose the correct verbs to complete the fable.

Verb Tenses

Once upon a time, a miser **hid** **hides** his gold at the foot of a tree in a biosphere (a special zone for living things). But he **didn't leave** **will leave** it there. Every week, he **digs** **dug** it up, just to look at it.

But the old miser wasn't the only one who **looks** **looked** at his gold. One day, a thief **will see** **saw** him with it! So the thief came back and **steals** **stole** it all.

When the old miser discovered his gold was gone, he made such a ruckus that all his neighbors **will come** **came** outside.

"Did you ever use the gold?" one asked him.

"No," he said. "I only looked at it."

"Then look at the hole that the thief left," the neighbor said. "It will do you just as much good."

Upon completion, add this sticker to your path on the map!

Brain Box

The **past tense** describes things that already happened, the **present tense** describes things that are happening now, and the **future tense** describes things that will happen.

Can It Be Reversed?

Look at each picture, and write whether the situation is **reversible** or **irreversible**.

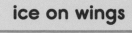

ice on wings

melted metal

mixed paint

thick mist on windows

Brain Box

If a change can be undone, it is called a **reversible change**. For example, ice can melt, then freeze again. But if the change cannot be undone, it is called an **irreversible change**. For example, if you cook an egg, the egg cannot be uncooked.

Reversible and Irreversible Changes

Upon completion, add these stickers to your path on the map!

melted popsicle

[ ]

steam

[ ]

toasted bread

[ ]

BONUS: An ice-covered asteroid orbits close to the sun and then far from the sun. What reversible change could happen? Explain your answer.

_____

_____

_____

_____

_____

Now add this sticker to your map!

Deep Space Snacks

Draw a line to split the fruit snack in half.
Then write the number name for one part.

$\dfrac{1}{2}$

Draw two lines to split the snack in thirds.
Then write the number name for one part.

Brain Box

Fractions show parts of a whole.
They can be written in words
(one-half) or as a figure ($\frac{1}{2}$).

Fractions

Draw two or three lines to split each snack into fourths. Then write the number name for one part.

Fractions

Draw your favorite food. Divide it into fourths and write the fraction for one part.

Characters

Paul Bunyan in Space

Read the story. Then answer each question with complete sentences.

Paul Bunyan was a giant of a man who had already accomplished a lot on Earth. When he couldn't find a watering hole big enough for his best friend, Babe the Blue Ox, he dug five new ones: the Great Lakes. One day, when he needed to put out a fire, he piled rocks on the cinders and created Mount Hood in Oregon. But it had been a long time since those adventures, and he was looking for a new challenge.

So when the first rocket was ready to be shot into space, the president called Paul. "We want to see what it's like out there in space," the president told him. "Will you hitch a ride on our rocket and take a look around?" So when the rocket was launched into space, Paul was hanging on. "I'm glad you're here," the Man in the Moon said when Paul arrived in space. "I've got an itch that I can't scratch, because I don't have any hands. Can you help me?" At first Paul tried to use a feather from the tail of the Swan constellation, but that only made the Moon giggle. Meanwhile, Babe had been making friends with the Ram. "Here, use my horn," the Ram said. So Paul picked him up, horns and all, and used him to scratch the Moon's nose. Along the way, the Ram's horns dug some holes in the moon. And that's how the Moon got its craters.

Brain Box

A **folktale** is a story that people pass on by telling it over and over again. It isn't written by a single author.

What did the president do to find out what's in space?

_____

_____

Why do you think Paul Bunyan accepted the president's challenge?

_____

_____

What did the Man in the Moon do when his nose became itchy?

_____

_____

What was Paul's first solution to this challenge?

_____

_____

What did Paul do when his first idea didn't work out?

_____

_____

BONUS: Paul Bunyan next meets Andromeda, a princess and constellation. She is chained to the sky and wants to be free. Based on the story above, do you think Paul Bunyan would help her? Make a prediction and write a short story.

_____

_____

_____

_____

_____

_____

_____

_____

Characters

Upon completion, add these stickers to your path on the map!

Now add this sticker to your map!

Rows and Columns

Count the number in each row. Then fill in the missing numbers to find the total.

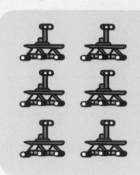

How many rovers are there?

2 + ☐ + ☐ = ☐ **rovers**

How many space aliens are there?

☐ + ☐ + ☐ + ☐ + ☐ = ☐ **space aliens**

How many comets are there?

☐ + ☐ + ☐ = ☐ **comets**

How many rockets are there?

☐ + ☐ + ☐ + ☐ = ☐ **rockets**

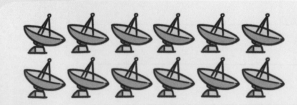

How many telescopes are there?

☐ + ☐ = ☐ **telescopes**

Level 6 complete!

Add this achievement sticker
to your path…

…and move on to

Level 7

on page 106!

Star Clusters

Count the number of equal groups. Fill in the missing numbers to find the products.

Equal Groups

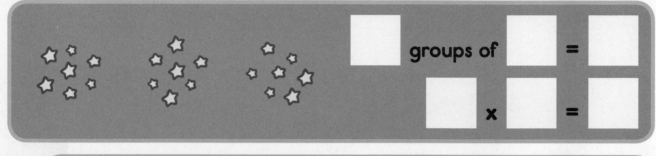

2 groups of 6 = 12

2 x 6 = 12

_____ groups of _____ = _____

_____ x _____ = _____

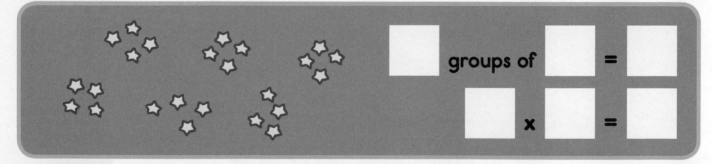

_____ groups of _____ = _____

_____ x _____ = _____

_____ groups of _____ = _____

_____ x _____ = _____

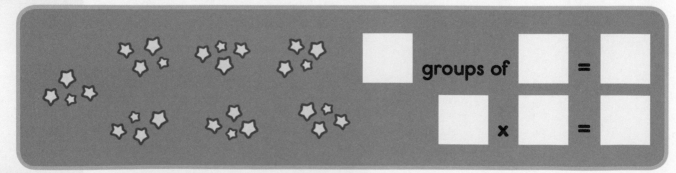

_____ groups of _____ = _____

_____ x _____ = _____

Brain Box

The multiplication symbol (x) means join equal groups.

Planet Pops

Divide these planet pops equally. Draw circles to make equal groups. Then solve each equation.

Equal Groups

Share 16 Earth pops equally among 2 people. How many pops does each person get?

16 ÷ 2 = [ ] **pops**

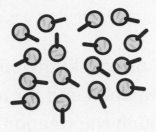

Share 30 Saturn pops equally among 5 people. How many pops does each person get?

30 ÷ 5 = [ ] **pops**

Share 20 Venus pops equally among 5 people. How many pops does each person get?

20 ÷ 5 = [ ] **pops**

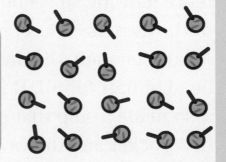

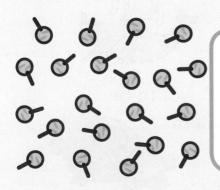

Share 21 Jupiter pops equally among 7 people. How many pops does each person get?

21 ÷ 7 = [ ] **pops**

Share 18 Mercury pops equally among 3 people. How many pops does each person get?

18 ÷ 3 = [ ] **pops**

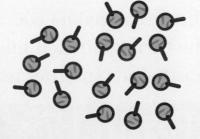

Brain Box

The division symbol (÷) means separate into equal groups.

How Did Thor Get His Hammer?

Read this old Norse story. Then answer each question using complete sentences.

Main Idea and Conclusions

Thor was known for his giant hammer. He used it as a weapon and for important ceremonies and blessings. Although the weapon became precious to him, he received it from a trickster named Loki after a few mean tricks.

One day, Loki, the trickster, was in the mood for mischief. So he cut off all the beautiful gold hair of Sif, Thor's wife. Of course, Thor was furious. But when Thor grabbed Loki, he begged Thor not to hurt him. He offered to go ask the dwarfs, who could make anything, to make more hair for Sif. Thor agreed, so Loki set off for the land of the dwarfs.

Sure enough, the dwarf Ivaldi fashioned a new head of hair for Sif. But he didn't stop there. He also made a ship that could be folded up and put in a pocket and the world's deadliest spear.

But Loki wasn't satisfied with these incredible gifts. So he taunted two other dwarf craftsmen: "I bet *you* can't make anything as good as what Ivaldi just made!" Not to be outdone, those dwarfs began making a golden boar and a gold ring that made new rings. But as they were finishing their creations, Loki realized he was about to lose his bet! So he turned himself into a fly and began to bite the craftsmen in order to distract them.

Brain Box

A **myth** is a traditional story that often explains the early history of a people or a natural wonder. Norse mythology is a collection of tales from ancient Scandinavia, which includes the countries of Denmark, Norway, and Sweden.

One of the craftsmen was also working on the best hammer in the world. The hammer never missed when it was thrown, and it came back to its owner like a boomerang when it was done. The hammer was nearly complete when Loki's bite startled the craftsman and he was too hurt to continue. So the handle turned out just a little too short.

Despite the flawed handle, the other dwarf craftsmen proved that they were just as good as Ivaldi because when Thor received the hammer, it became his most prized possession. He realized its power, and from that day on he took it everywhere. And now his hammer is just as famous as he is.

Main Idea and Conclusions

Upon completion, add these stickers to your path on the map!

What is the first thing that happens in this story?

_____

_____

How does Thor feel about this event? Use a detail from the text that shows his feelings.

_____

_____

Which character speaks the one line of dialogue in this story?

_____

What are the dwarfs good at?

_____

What is the main question that this story answers?

_____

_____

What happens at the end of this story?

_____

_____

Reading Clues

Draw a line to match each plant or animal to its fossil.

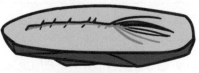

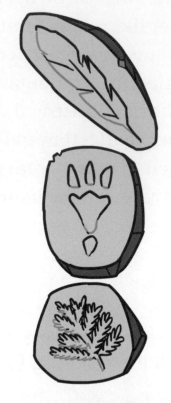

Upon completion, add this sticker to your path on the map!

Brain Box

A **fossil** is the remains, or impression marks, left behind by a prehistoric plant or animal. Plant and animal fossils often occur near rivers, ponds, and lakes. For example, plant parts fall or are washed into bodies of water and become buried under layers of dirt. If more dirt is layered on top, the pressure will make the fossil's impression.

Write about and draw what fossils this fern may leave in the future.

_____

_____

My Spaceship

Design your own spaceship using quadrilaterals and triangles. Use at least one triangle, one square, one rectangle, one rhombus, and one quadrilateral that does not belong to any of these categories.

My Name: Captain _____

My Ship's Name: _____

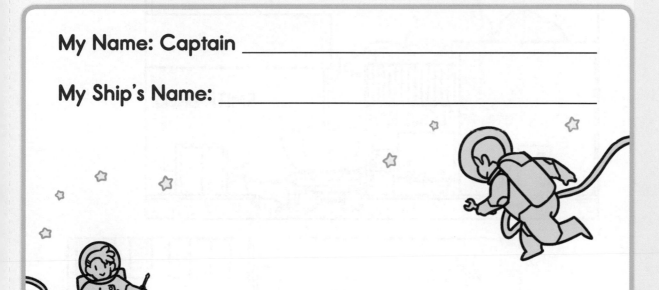

Upon completion, add this sticker to your path on the map!

Continuity and Change

What's the Difference?

Take a look at both pictures. Circle each object in the present that has changed as time passed.

Brain Box

By comparing the past with the present, we can better understand how societies behave and change over time. This knowledge can help explain current problems and perhaps lead people to find solutions.

BONUS: Why do you think the flag stayed the same through time?

_____

Choose one item that changed and one item that stayed the same. Why do you think it changed? Why do you think it stayed the same?

_____

_____

_____

_____

Now add this sticker to your map!

Connect the Stars

Complete each sentence with a linking word or phrase from the box.

Linking Words

therefore and because also but for example

They couldn't go outside _____ there was a meteor storm.

The comet shot out next to Neptune _____ headed toward the sun.

Penny begged her mom to let her go to Mars, _____ her mom said no.

Jian wanted to visit Pluto, and _____ Ceres.

It is rare that planets align; _____ Mars, Mercury, Venus, Jupiter, Saturn, and the moon will only align again in 2040!

The scientist concluded, _____, that the meteor was headed straight for Earth.

Brain Box

Linking words or phrases are used to connect more than one idea.

Upon completion, add this sticker to your path on the map!

Write a sentence about the picture to the left with one of the linking words above.

_____

_____

_____

Moon Fractions

What part of each moon is shown? Fill in the missing parts of the fraction to answer.

This is $\dfrac{1}{4}$  What fraction is this?  $\dfrac{}{4}$

This is $\dfrac{1}{3}$  What fraction is this?  $\dfrac{}{3}$

This is $\dfrac{1}{6}$ What fraction is this?  $\dfrac{}{6}$

This is $\dfrac{1}{8}$  What fraction is this?  $\dfrac{}{8}$

Each part of the moon is $\dfrac{1}{4}$.

Color $\dfrac{3}{4}$ of the moon.

Planet Peril

Erosion is what happens when wind or water changes the shape of land. Read about how to prevent erosion. Then answer each question.

Dikes

Dikes are walls built to keep the sea from flooding the land. Dikes can be natural or man-made. People often create dikes with sandbags. Sand absorbs water and lets very little water through.

Natural Hazards

Lightning Rod

A lightning rod is a metal rod attached to a tall building. Lightning will strike the rod and travel down a wire to channel the electricity safely into the ground.

Upon completion, add this sticker to your path on the map!

Hedges

A hedge is a group of sturdy plants that form a boundary or fence. The strong plants that form a hedge can block wind and shelter yards.

What can keep an ocean-side city from sinking into the sea? Explain how.

_____

_____

What can keep a tall building from being damaged during a lightning storm? Explain how.

_____

_____

What can protect gardens from wind? Explain how.

_____

_____

Space Junk

Read each word problem. Then draw a picture and write an equation to solve.

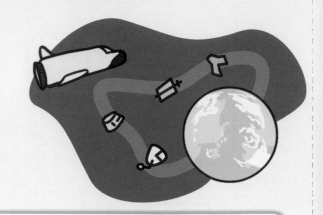

Two robots gathered 9 pieces of space junk each. How many pieces of space junk did they have altogether?

_____ **pieces**

The robots then separated their junk into 3 equal groups. How many pieces were in each group?

_____ **pieces**

If 6 space dogs were given 5 bones each, what is the total number of bones the dogs were given?

_____ **bones**

Forty-eight meteors fell to the earth over 8 days. If an equal amount fell each day, how many meteors fell each day?

_____ **meteors**

Alien Agreement

Circle the word that correctly completes each sentence.

Pronoun Antecedent Agreement

The Tigs and the Tugs never get along at **his** **their** yearly barbecue. The Tigs think Mr. Tug makes **his** **their** sauce too spicy. The Tugs think Mrs. Tig adds too much sugar to **her** **their** lemonade.

But **everybody** **anybody** loves the Tig-Tug ice cream. Mr. Tug knows half of the recipe, and Mrs. Tig has the other half in **her** **their** head. Nobody could make **it** **them** alone, so everyone keeps getting together. "It's delicious!" **they** **she** all agree.

Upon completion, add this sticker to your path on the map!

Rounding Tens
and Hundreds

Around the Universe

Each planet takes a different number of days to orbit its star. Round each number of days to the nearest ten.

67 days ≈ __70__ days

35 days ≈ _____ days

31 days ≈ _____ days

12 days ≈ _____ days

88 days ≈ _____ days

54 days ≈ _____ days

23 days ≈ _____ days

19 days ≈ _____ days

46 days ≈ _____ days

92 days ≈ _____ days

Brain Box

To **round to the nearest ten**, find the number in the ones place. If the number is **5** or greater, round up. If the number is **4** or less, round down.

Round each number of days to the nearest hundred.

373 days ≈ __400__ days

406 days ≈ _____ days

159 days ≈ _____ days

555 days ≈ _____ days

836 days ≈ _____ days

490 days ≈ _____ days

Upon completion, add these stickers to your path on the map!

777 days ≈ _____ days

225 days ≈ _____ days

Brain Box

To **round to the nearest hundred,** find the number in the tens place. If the number is **5** or greater, round up. If the number is **4** or less, round down.

Able and Baker were two monkeys who flew to about 360 miles above Earth. Could the exact height be 363 miles? Why or why not?

_____

_____

_____

CONGRATULATIONS!
You completed all of your math quests! You earned:

Analyzing
Data

Which Works Better?

Obi and Tobi each designed a machine to make spaceberry pancakes. Read the data from their breakfast test, and answer each question.

Brain Box

Data is the information you get when you do research or run a test.

	OBI	TOBI
Pancakes Made per Minute	2	4
Pancakes Burned per Minute	1	3
Cups of Wasted Pancake Batter	2	1
Fluffiness of Pancakes (5 = fluffy, 1 = not fluffy)	5	3

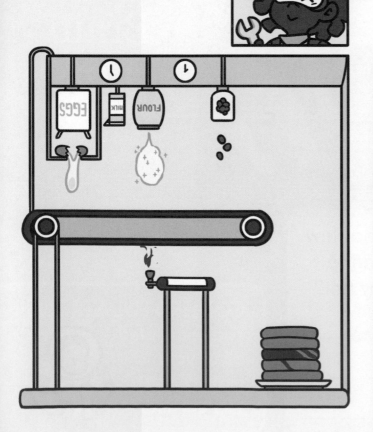

Analyzing Data

Whose machine made the most pancakes per minute?

_____

Whose machine wasted the most batter?

_____

Whose machine burned the most pancakes?

_____

Whose machine made the fluffiest pancakes?

_____

If you throw away the burned pancakes, how many good pancakes did Obi's machine make per minute?

_____

If you throw away the burned pancakes, how many good pancakes did Tobi's machine make per minute?

_____

Whose machine made the most pancakes that weren't burned, with the least batter wasted?

_____

What do you think is a strength of Obi's machine?

_____

_____

What do you think is a strength of Tobi's machine?

_____

_____

Upon completion, add these stickers to your path on the map!

CONGRATULATIONS! You completed all of your science quests! You earned:

Key Details

Who? What? Where?

Read the fable. Then answer each question.

Country Mouse and City Mouse

One day, City Mouse went to visit his cousin in the country, far from Cosmic City. His cousin, Country Mouse, wasn't fancy, but he loved his city cousin. All Country Mouse had to offer were Big Dipper beans, comet cheese, and potatoes from Pluto, but he offered them freely.

City Mouse turned up his nose at the country fare. "I can't understand how you eat food like this," he said. "But what can you expect in the country? Come to Cosmic City with me! You'll never want to return here."

The two mice set off by rocket for the city and arrived that night.

"You must be hungry after the trip," the City Mouse said. So he took his cousin to a grand dining room. They found the remains of a feast, and dined on moon pie crumbs and space jam.

Suddenly, they heard growling and barking.

"What is that?" asked Country Mouse.

"It is only the dogs of the house," City Mouse told him.

"Only!" said Country Mouse. "I do *not* like that as music during dinner."

The door to the dining room flew open. Two giant space dogs dashed in.

City Mouse and Country Mouse scrambled to escape.

"Good-bye, Cousin," Country Mouse said.

"Are you going so soon?" City Mouse asked.

"Yes," Country Mouse said. "Better beans and potatoes in peace than moon pies in fear."

Who visited Country Mouse?

_____

What did Country Mouse serve City Mouse to eat?

_____

_____

Where did City Mouse and Country Mouse go together?

_____

When did they arrive?

_____

Why did City Mouse think Country Mouse would like the city?

_____

How did Country Mouse and City Mouse realize there were dogs nearby?

_____

What did Country Mouse mean when he said, "Better beans and potatoes in peace than moon pies in fear?"

_____

_____

_____

Key Details

Upon completion, add these stickers to your path on the map!

BONUS: Imagine that City Mouse takes Country Mouse on a helicopter ride over Cosmic City. Write a few sentences to describe where they might go and what they might see.

_____

_____

_____

_____

_____

Now add this sticker to your map!

The Space Age Begins

Read about the space race. Then write the title of each event and the date in the correct place on the timeline below.

Timelines

SPUTNIK 1

On October 4, 1957, the former Soviet Union sent *Sputnik 1* into orbit. It was the first man-made satellite (a satellite can be any object in orbit around a planet—in fact, our moon is a natural satellite). The success of *Sputnik 1* started the "Space Race"—a race between the Soviet Union and the United States to be the first to put a man on the moon.

SPUTNIK 2

The Soviet Union launched *Sputnik 2* soon after, on November 3, 1957—this time, with a dog named Laika inside! This was the first satellite to carry a life-form. Meanwhile, the U.S. hadn't yet launched a thing.

EXPLORER 1

On January 31, 1958, the Americans began to catch up and launched *Explorer 1*. The satellite not only reached orbit, but also gathered useful scientific information.

NASA

President Dwight Eisenhower announced a new government-run agency that would explore space. On July 29, 1958, the National Aeronautics and Space Administration (NASA) was born!

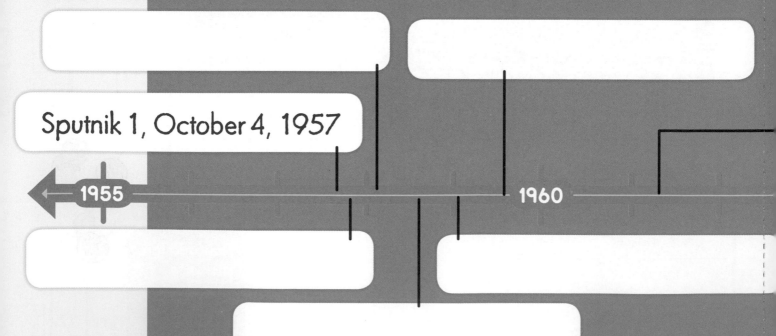

Sputnik 1, October 4, 1957

1955

1960

LUNA 1

The Soviets nearly reached the moon on January 2, 1959, with their spacecraft *Luna 1*. However, it missed its mark! As a result, it was the first spacecraft to leave the orbit of Earth.

LUNA 2

Luna 2 was the first spacecraft to successfully reach the moon's surface. It took around 34 hours to get there, and crash-landed on September 14, 1959. Luckily, no one was inside! The Soviets were still in the lead.

FIRST MAN IN SPACE

Yuri Gagarin became the first man in space on April 12, 1961. His spacecraft, *Vostok 1*, circled around the earth and landed about two hours after it had launched. Gagarin parachuted out of his spacecraft before it crash-landed.

FIRST WOMAN IN SPACE

Just two years later, on June 16, 1963, Valentina Tereshkova became the first woman in space.

A MAN ON THE MOON

It wasn't until six years later that the U.S. was able to land a man on the moon. On July 20, 1969, *Apollo 11* landed, and Neil Armstrong became the first man to walk on the moon. The U.S. had won the space race!

1965 ———————————————————— 1970 →

CONGRATULATIONS!

You completed all of your social studies quests! You earned:

How Was Your Summer?

Fill in your opinion about summer vacation.
Provide reasons to support your opinion.

Opinions

Upon
completion,
add this
sticker to
your path on
the map!

I believe that summer vacation is _____

_____ because

_____.

I really like to _____ during the

summer because _____.

There are lots of _____

_____ during the summer, too.

Also, I never have to _____ during

the summer because _____.

Everyone should think that summer vacation is

_____ because

_____.

In conclusion, I think that summer vacation is

_____ because

_____.

Brain Box

Persuasive writing tries to get the reader to
agree with an **opinion** or point of view.

Authors use **supporting facts**—true information
or reasons that support the opinion.

CONGRATULATIONS!
You completed all of your
English language
arts quests!
You earned:

Quest complete!

Add this achievement sticker to your path...

...and turn to the next page for your Summer Brainiac Award!

Summer Brainiac Award!

You have completed your entire Summer Brain Quest! Woo-hoo! Congratulations! That's quite an achievement.

Write your name on the line and cut out the award certificate. Show your friends. Hang it on your wall! You're a certified Summer Brainiac!

Summer Brainiac Award

Presented to:

_____

for successfully completing the learning journey in

SUMMER BRAIN QUEST®: BETWEEN GRADES 2&3

Outside Quests

This is not just a workbook—it's a trip into the past, a visit from aliens, a way to enjoy the summer sunshine, and so much more! Summer is the perfect time to explore the great outdoors. Use the Outside Quests to make your next sunny day more fun than ever—and earn an achievement sticker.

Outside
Quests

Level 1 — Pebble Toss Addition

Find a partner, a pebble, and some chalk. Draw 9 connected squares on the ground and write the digits from 1 to 9 (one digit in each square). Toss a pebble onto the number squares trying to get the pebble to land in the square with the largest digit. Then toss a second pebble. Make the largest number you can with the two digits by adding or multiplying. Next, it's your partner's turn. Whoever makes the largest number wins.

Now add this sticker to your map!

Level 3 — Point of View

Find your favorite object in your neighborhood or yard. Write a paragraph about how it would look to an alien from another planet. What would they notice, what would surprise them, and why?

Now add this sticker to your map!

Level 3 — My Environment

Pick a spot outside and observe your environment. Write "field notes" about the following: weather, temperature, plant life, animal life, soil/foundation, sounds, and smells. Note if there is anything else you notice and what is unique about your environment.

Now add this sticker to your map!

Level 5 — Map Your Favorite Place

Go to your favorite place outside and draw a map of it. For example, your map might include a swing set, bench, playing field, goalpost, hill, trees, and more. Look around and draw objects that are important to you.

Now add this sticker to your map!

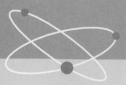

Outside
Quests

Now add
this sticker
to your
map!

Level 5A — You're in the News

Take a walk around your neighborhood. Then write a headline and news story about what's happening there today. Or write a headline and a news story about what you *wish* was going on in your neighborhood today.

Level 5A — Past and Present

Go outside and make a list of 5 things that you think have been there for over 50 years. Make a list of 5 things that you think have been there for less than a year.

Now add
this sticker
to your
map!

Level 6 — Map of the Stars

Go outside and look at the stars. Choose one group of at least 5 stars that stands out to you, and draw a map of it. Then create your own constellation: Decide what it looks like to you and connect the stars any way you like. Last, name your constellation!

Now add this sticker to your map!

Level 7 — Shape Scavenger Hunt

Go for a walk and look for shapes around you and name them. Try to find a quadrilateral that is not a square or a rectangle. After your walk, use sidewalk chalk to draw the different quadrilaterals that you saw.

Now add this sticker to your map!

Answer Key

(For pages not included in this section,
answers will vary.)

3, 2, 1…Blast Off!
Complete each word using a prefix or a suffix.

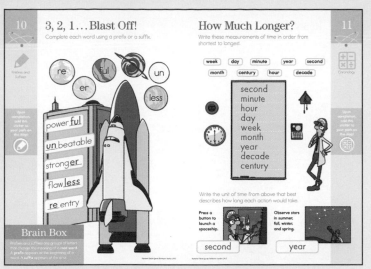

Prefixes: re, er, ful, un, less

power**ful**
unbeatable
strong**er**
flaw**less**
reentry

Brain Box
Prefixes and suffixes are groups of letters that change the meaning of a root word. A prefix appears at the beginning of a word. A suffix appears at the end.

How Much Longer?
Write these measurements of time in order from shortest to longest.

| week | day | minute | year | second |
| month | century | hour | decade |

second
minute
hour
day
week
month
year
decade
century

Write the unit of time from above that best describes how long each action would take.

Press a button to launch a spaceship. → **second**

Observe stars in summer, fall, winter, and spring. → **year**

Cloud Counting
Is the number of birds in each cloud an even or odd amount? Circle each pair of birds. Then write the number of birds in each cloud and whether it is even or odd.

13 odd
16 even
25 odd
22 even

Brain Box
An even number is a whole number that ends in 0, 2, 4, 6, or 8. An even number of objects makes pairs. An odd number is a whole number that ends in 1, 3, 5, 7, or 9. An odd number of objects does not make pairs.

Swift or Slow Science
Write whether each event happens suddenly or gradually.

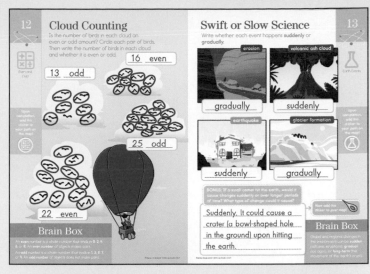

erosion → gradually
volcanic ash cloud → suddenly
earthquake → suddenly
glacier formation → gradually

BONUS: If a small comet hit the earth, would it cause changes suddenly or over longer periods of time? What type of change could it cause?

Suddenly. It could cause a crater (a bowl-shaped hole in the ground) upon hitting the earth.

Families in the Sky
Add or subtract to complete the equations in each fact family.

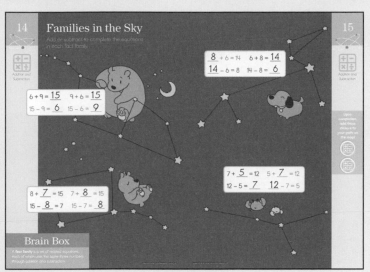

$8 + 6 = 14$ $6 + 8 = 14$
$14 - 6 = 8$ $14 - 8 = 6$

$6 + 9 = 15$ $9 + 6 = 15$
$15 - 9 = 6$ $15 - 6 = 9$

$7 + 5 = 12$ $5 + 7 = 12$
$12 - 5 = 7$ $12 - 7 = 5$

$8 + 7 = 15$ $7 + 8 = 15$
$15 - 8 = 7$ $15 - 7 = 8$

Brain Box
A fact family is a set of related equations, each of which uses the same three numbers through addition and subtraction.

Where in the World?
Fill in the missing commas in each sentence.

The desert-dwelling Arzauns are comet jumpers, which means they travel by comet.

To catch a ride on a comet, they use a strong lasso.

They wait for comets to swing by, then loop their rope around them and hop on!

Arzauns call comets "dirty snowballs" because they contain dust, ice, gases, and more.

Comets travel fast, like spaceships, but they are hard to steer.

However, unlike a spaceship, you can't just stop a comet anywhere you want.

Brain Box
A comma is used to indicate a pause in a sentence and to separate words in a list of three or more things.

17

Fill in the missing apostrophes in each sentence.

So Arzauns don't always know where they'll wind up!

Fortunately, Arzauns don't mind.

They're always up for exploring someone else's world.

That's because Arzauns have a superpower: Wherever they go, they can always make friends.

So wherever they land, they're glad to be there!

Brain Box
A contraction is two words that are joined together. When the two words are joined, some of the letters in the second word are replaced by an apostrophe. For example, I + am becomes I'm. To make a singular noun or a word made possessive by adding an apostrophe. For example, Halley's comet or the Arzaun's lasso.

18

What in the World?
Answer each question using one of the words from the box.

| sight | stick | thermometer |
| touch | scale | notebook |

Which is the best tool to find out the weight of a meteorite? → scale

Which is the best tool to find out how hot a meteorite is? → thermometer

Which is the best sense to use to find out the color of a meteorite? → sight

Which is the best tool to record what you see, touch, and smell? → notebook

Which is the best tool to find out if a meteorite is soft or hard without touching it with your hand? → stick

Which is the best sense to use to find out whether a meteorite is rough or smooth? → touch

Brain Box
Observation is the act of noticing and gathering information about something. An observation can include the color, texture, hardness, and flexibility of something you are observing. Observation is the basis of all science.

20

Double Desert
Write the plural form of each word. Then circle the plural form in the word search. Words go across and down.

star → stars
dune → dunes
hat → hats
bush → bushes
camel → camels
tale → tales
grass → grasses
lamp → lamps
fox → foxes
mirage → mirages

```
D U N E S O I L C A W
V Z H A T S B A M A Y
P F S Z J N H L A W B
G R A S S E S P M B S
F B Q P E J M S E S T
E L N B U S H E S L A
T A L E S I H W G R
P C Q M I R A G E S
B O X I B F O X E S
```

Brain Box
Plural means more than one. Add an s to a single word to make it plural. Add an es if the noun ends in sh, ch, s, or x.

One Thousand Miles
To fill in the missing highway signs, count by tens on one side and hundreds on the other.

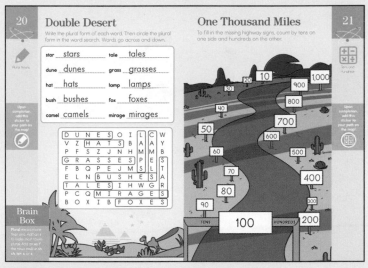

10, 20, 30, 40, 50, 60, 70, 80, 90, 100 (TENS)
100, 200, 300, 400, 500, 600, 700, 800, 900, 1,000 (HUNDREDS)

Where's the Water?
Label the events in the water cycle below as condensation, precipitation, collection, or evaporation.

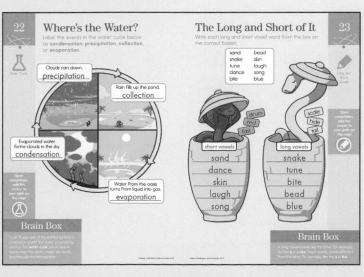

Clouds rain down. → precipitation
Rain fills up the pond. → collection
Evaporated water forms clouds in the sky. → condensation
Water from the oasis turns from liquid into gas. → evaporation

Brain Box
Over 70 percent of the earth's surface is covered in water. This water is constantly moving. The water cycle shows how water travels from the oasis, over the earth, under the earth, and through the atmosphere.

The Long and Short of It
Write each long and short vowel word from the box on the correct basket.

sand, bead, snake, skin, tune, laugh, dance, song, bite, blue
drum, red, fast, scale, hide, time

short vowels:
sand
dance
skin
laugh
song

long vowels:
snake
tune
bite
bead
blue

Brain Box
A long sound sounds like the letter, for example: the i in snake. A short sound sounds different from the letter, for example, the a in bat.

Read the Clues
Answer each question using the information provided on the map.

MAP KEY
gold mine
farm
government building
palace

Brain Box
A map is a picture or chart of something, like the earth's surface. A key or legend explains the most pictures or symbols on the map.

Which city is farther north: Biri or Diri? → Biri

Which city is farthest west? → Miri

How many cities are NOT on a river? → Two

Which city is closer to Iri: Biri or Diri? → Biri

Where might people in Iri get most of their food? → From Biri and Diri

What are two possible reasons why Iri is the biggest city on the map? → Answers will vary. Sample answer: Iri has the most water and the palace, so it could draw and support many people.

Why might someone choose to live in Miri, when it is so far away from water? → Miri has gold.

What might people in Miri need from people in Iri, Biri, and Diri? → Water, food, or government services

What might people in Iri, Biri, and Diri want from Miri? → Gold

BONUS: You're in Miri, and bandits are robbing the gold mine! How many miles do you need to travel to get help and which city do you go to? → 15 miles, Iri

26

Radio Waves

Broadcast each number by writing each digit in the correct place on the chart.

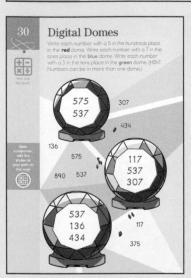

	Hundreds	Tens	Ones
157	1	5	7
200	2	0	0
823	8	2	3
68		6	8
375	3	7	5
240	2	4	0

Hundreds	Tens	Ones	
3	0	0	300
7	6	6	766
4	0	5	405
	7	9	79
1	9	0	190

Brain Box

You can use **place value** to figure out how much numbers are worth. If you see three numbers, you know that the number is made up of hundreds, tens, and ones. 3-624 is made are 6 hundreds, 2 tens, and 4 ones.

Hundreds	Tens	Ones
6	2	4

BONUS: The tower broadcasts a number that has 1 in the tens place, 4 in the ones place, and 9 in the hundreds place. What number is it? 914

28

Risky Riddles

Read the story from Greek mythology. Then answer each question.

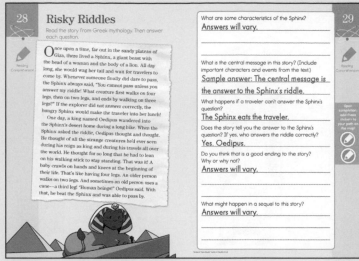

Once upon a time, far out in the sandy plateau of Giza, there lived a Sphinx, a giant beast with the head of a woman and the body of a lion. All day long, she would wag her tail and wait for travelers to come by. Whenever someone finally did dare to pass, the Sphinx always said, "You cannot pass unless you answer my riddle! What creature first walks on four legs, then on two legs, and ends by walking on three legs?" If the explorer did not answer correctly, the hungry Sphinx would make the traveler into her lunch!

One day, a king named Oedipus wandered into the Sphinx's desert home during a long hike. When the Sphinx asked the riddle, Oedipus thought and thought. He thought of all the strange creatures he'd ever seen during his reign as king and during his travels all over the world. He thought for so long that he had to lean on his walking stick to stay standing. That was it! A baby crawls on hands and knees at the beginning of their life. That's like having four legs. An older person walks on two legs. And sometimes an old person uses a cane—a third leg! "Human beings!" Oedipus said. With that, he beat the Sphinx and was able to pass by.

29

What are some characteristics of the Sphinx?
Answers will vary.

What is the central message in this story? (Include important characters and events from the text.)
Sample answer: The central message is the answer to the Sphinx's riddle.

What happens if a traveler can't answer the Sphinx's question?
The Sphinx eats the traveler.

Does the story tell you the answer to the Sphinx's question? If yes, who answers the riddle correctly?
Yes. Oedipus.

Do you think that is a good ending to the story? Why or why not?
Answers will vary.

What might happen in a sequel to this story?
Answers will vary.

30

Digital Domes

Write each number with a 5 in the hundreds place in the **red** dome. Write each number with a 7 in the ones place in the **blue** dome. Write each number with a 3 in the tens place in the **green** dome. (HINT: Numbers can be in more than one dome.)

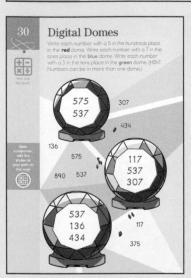

575 537 307 434 136 575 537 890 117 537 307 537 136 434 117 375

Red dome: 575 537
Blue dome: 117 537 307
Green dome: 537 136 434

32

Sky Woman's Power

Many native people call North America **Turtle Island**. Number each passage of the story in the correct sequence to learn why.

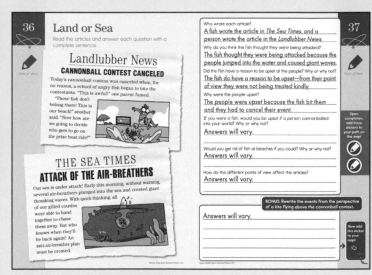

2 But Sky Woman had a special power. If she had even a small bit of earth, she could make more earth. Enough for everyone to live on.

6 Sky Woman placed the earth on a turtle's back. Then she used her powers to make more and more land—until the tiny bit of earth grew into what is now called North America!

4 One by one, each animal dove, but none of them reached the bottom. Finally, only the tiny muskrat was left.

3 However, there was no earth to be found! So Sky Woman asked all the animals to dive to the bottom of the ocean and bring some earth back up to the surface.

1 Once, a great flood covered the world. Sky Woman came down to Earth, but there was no place for her to rest—just miles and miles of water, all over.

5 The muskrat was gone all day and all night. But in the morning, his furry whiskers broke the surface of the water, and after a deep breath, he offered his paw filled with a tiny bit of earth!

BONUS: How does Sky Woman remake the world?
She puts a piece of land on the back of the turtle and uses her power to make more land.

33

Word Magic

Match words in each column to create a **compound word**. Then write the compound word.

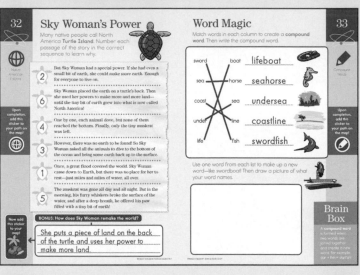

sword — boat — **lifeboat**
sea — horse — **seahorse**
coast — sea — **undersea**
under — line — **coastline**
life — fish — **swordfish**

Use one word from each list to make up a new word—like swordboat! Then draw a picture of what your word names.

Brain Box

A compound word is formed when two words are joined together to create a new word. For example: sea + fish = starfish!

Hundreds of Leagues Under the Sea

Write the **standard form** of the number that is described on each banner.

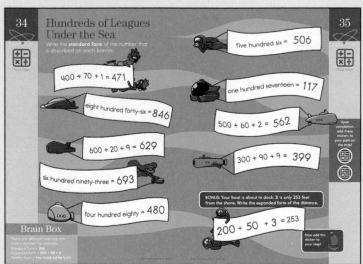

five hundred six = 506
400 + 70 + 1 = 471
one hundred seventeen = 117
eight hundred forty-six = 846
500 + 60 + 2 = 562
600 + 20 + 9 = 629
300 + 90 + 9 = 399
six hundred ninety-three = 693
four hundred eighty = 480

BONUS: Your boat is about to dock. It is only 253 feet from the shore. Write the expanded form of the distance.
200 + 50 + 3 = 253

Brain Box

There are different ways you can write a number. For example:
Standard Form: 246
Expanded Form: 200 + 40 + 6
Written Form: two hundred forty-six

Land or Sea

Read the articles and answer each question with a complete sentence.

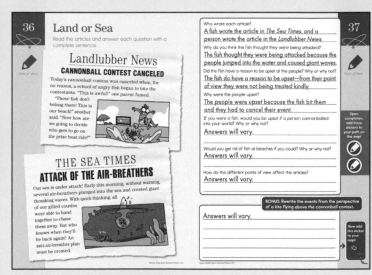

Landlubber News
CANNONBALL CONTEST CANCELED

Today's cannonball contest was canceled when, for no reason, a school of angry fish began to bite the contestants. "This is awful!" one parent fumed. "Those fish don't belong there! This is our beach!" another said. "Now how are we going to decide who gets to go on the prize boat ride!"

THE SEA TIMES
ATTACK OF THE AIR-BREATHERS

Our sea is under attack! Early this morning, without warning, several air-breathers plunged into the sea and created giant thrashing waves. With quick thinking, all of our gilled cousins were able to band together to chase them away. But who knows when they'll be back again? An anti-air-breather plan must be created.

Who wrote each article?
A fish wrote the article in *The Sea Times*, and a person wrote the article in the *Landlubber News*.

Why do you think the fish thought they were being attacked?
The fish thought they were being attacked because the people jumped into the water and caused giant waves.

Did the fish have a reason to be upset at the people? Why or why not?
The fish do have a reason to be upset—from their point of view they were not being treated kindly.

Why were the people upset?
The people were upset because the fish bit them and they had to cancel their event.

If you were a fish, would you be upset if a person cannonballed into your world? Why or why not?
Answers will vary.

Would you get rid of fish at beaches if you could? Why or why not?
Answers will vary.

How do the different points of view affect the articles?
Answers will vary.

BONUS: Rewrite the events from the perspective of a kite flying above the cannonball contest.
Answers will vary.

So Many Stinkbugs

Look at the different stinkbugs. Then answer each question and explain your answers.

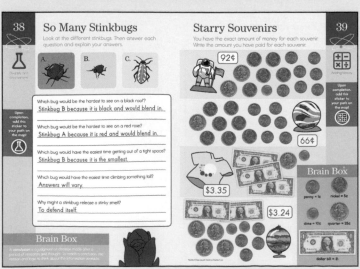

A.   B.   C.

Which bug would be the hardest to see on a black roof?
Stinkbug B because it is black and would blend in.

Which bug would be the hardest to see on a red rose?
Stinkbug A because it is red and would blend in.

Which bug would have the easiest time getting out of a tight space?
Stinkbug B because it is the smallest.

Which bug would have the easiest time climbing something tall?
Answers will vary.

Why might a stinkbug release a stinky smell?
To defend itself.

Brain Box

A conclusion is a judgment or decision made after a piece of research and thought. To reach a conclusion, use reason and logic to think about the information around you.

Starry Souvenirs

You have the exact amount of money for each souvenir. Write the amount you have paid for each souvenir.

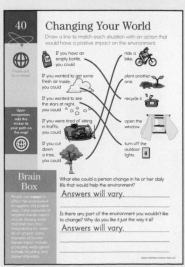

92¢
66¢
$3.35
$3.24

Brain Box

penny = 1¢   nickel = 5¢
dime = 10¢   quarter = 25¢
dollar bill = $1

Changing Your World

Draw a line to match each situation with an action that would have a positive impact on the environment.

If you have an empty bottle, you could — recycle it.
If you wanted to get some fresh air inside, you could — open the window.
If you wanted to see the stars at night, you could — turn off the outdoor lights.
If you were tired of sitting in traffic, you could — ride a bike.
If you cut down a tree, you could — plant another one.

Brain Box

People can impact or affect the environment in negative and positive ways. Some examples of negative human impact include: cutting down trees and polluting the water, air, or ground. Some examples of positive human impact include: protecting endangered animals, recycling, and conserving water.

What else could a person change in his or her daily life that would help the environment?
Answers will vary.

Is there any part of the environment you wouldn't like to change? Why do you like it just the way it is?
Answers will vary.

42

Space Adventure Camp

Compare the number of seconds each camper took to build a robot in a low-gravity simulator. Write <, =, or > in each circle.

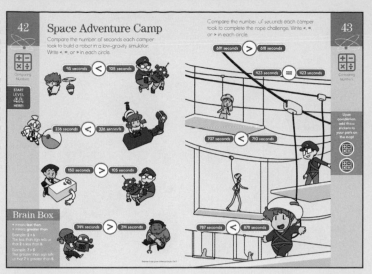

95 seconds < 105 seconds

236 seconds < 326 seconds

150 seconds > 105 seconds

344 seconds > 314 seconds

Brain Box

- < means less than.
- > means greater than.
- Example: 2 < 6. The less than sign tells us that 2 is less than 6.
- Example: 7 > 5. The greater than sign tells us that 7 is greater than 5.

Compare the number of seconds each camper took to complete the rope challenge. Write <, =, or > in each circle.

681 seconds > 618 seconds

423 seconds = 423 seconds

707 seconds < 710 seconds

787 seconds < 878 seconds

What Tools Do Astronauts Use?

Write which tool would best solve each problem.

small cutter • safety tether (rope) • wrench • robotic hands

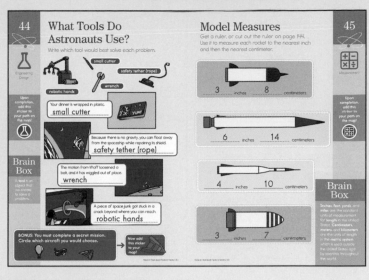

Your dinner is wrapped in plastic.
small cutter

Because there is no gravity, you can float away from the spaceship while repairing its shield.
safety tether (rope)

The motion from that loosened a bolt, and it has wiggled out of place.
wrench

A piece of space junk got stuck in a crack beyond where you can reach.
robotic hands

BONUS: You must complete a secret mission. Circle which aircraft you would choose.

Now add this sticker to your map!

Brain Box

A tool is an object that you choose to solve a problem.

45

Model Measures

Get a ruler, or cut out the ruler on page 144. Use it to measure each rocket to the nearest inch and then the nearest centimeter.

3 inches   8 centimeters

6 inches   14 centimeters

4 inches   10 centimeters

3 inches   7 centimeters

Brain Box

Inches, feet, yards, and miles are the standard units of measurement for length in the United States. Centimeters, meters, and kilometers are the units of length in the metric system, which is used outside the United States and by scientists throughout the world.

46

Satellite Sale!

Predict whether each event will lead to lower or higher prices of satellites. Write "lower prices" or "higher prices" next to each event.

BIG INCREASE IN THE PRICE OF STEEL FOR SATELLITES!
higher prices

lower prices

The machine broke and the part is on Mars! We can't make new satellites for months!
higher prices

Where are we going to put all these? The store is still full!
lower prices

Brain Box

Prices of goods usually go up when there's more demand. That means there is a lot of something that people want; for example, the price of bathing suits may go up during the summer because the demand increases.

Prices usually go down when there's plenty of supply. That means there is more of a good than people want to buy. For example, the price of footballs may go down if there are more footballs than football players.

BONUS: If someone invented a new satellite that's better than the old ones, would you expect the price of the old ones to go up or down?
down

Now add this sticker to your map!

Timely Takeoffs

Draw hands on each clock to show each launch time.

The space plane takes off at 2:00 p.m.

The spacecraft takes off at 6:55 a.m.

The spaceship takes off at 11:05 a.m.

The rocket takes off at 12:25 p.m.

Brain Box

An analog clock has three parts:
- A clock face
- A little hand that points to the hour
- A big hand that points to the minutes

Which Is Worse?

Each pair of words below has similar meanings. Circle the more negative descriptive word to complete each sentence.

"I'm cold (freezing)," Zim complained.

"Well, it's not my fault we're lost," Bim replied (snapped).

The two of them were unhappy (miserable) about being lost in space.

There had been (nothing) not much for them to eat for days.

Just when they thought they might be (starving) hungry, the Space Guard found them and towed them home.

"We never want to get delayed (stuck) like that again," they agreed.

Brain Box

Some words have several shades of meaning. The difference between them is called nuance.

BONUS: Write two adjectives that have similar meanings to describe an airplane.

Answers will vary.

Now add this sticker to your map!

Past, Present, and Future

Number each picture of the story in the correct sequence to learn how Johnny Appleseed made a difference in history. Then answer the question.

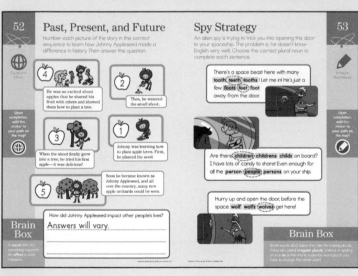

4 — He was so excited about apples that he shared his fruit with others and showed them how to plant a tree.

2 — Then, he watered the small shoot.

3 — When the shoot finally grew into a tree, he tried his first apple—it was delicious!

1 — Johnny was learning how to plant apple trees. First, he planted the seed.

5 — Soon he became known as Johnny Appleseed, and all over the country, many new apple orchards could be seen.

How did Johnny Appleseed impact other people's lives?
Answers will vary.

Brain Box

A cause tells why something happens. An effect is what happens.

Spy Strategy

An alien spy is trying to trick you into opening the door to your spaceship. The problem is, he doesn't know English very well. Choose the correct plural noun to complete each sentence.

There's a space beast here with many tooth, teeth, tooths! Let me in! He's just a few foots (feet) foot away from the door.

Are there (children) childrens childs on board? I have lots of candy to share! Even enough for all the person (people) persons on your ship.

Hurry up and open the door, before the space wolf, wolfs, (wolves) get here!

Brain Box

Some words don't follow the rules for making plurals. These are called irregular plurals. Instead of adding an s or es at the end to make the word plural, you have to change the whole word.

Nebula Popularity

Space campers vote for their favorite nebula (swirling clouds of gas and dust). Solve each word problem by adding or subtracting.

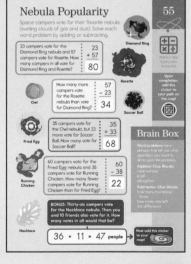

Diamond Ring
23 campers vote for the Diamond Ring nebula and 57 campers vote for Rosette. How many campers in all vote for Diamond Ring and Rosette?
$\begin{array}{r}23\\+57\\\hline 80\end{array}$

Rosette / Owl
How many more campers vote for the Rosette nebula than vote for Diamond Ring?
$\begin{array}{r}57\\-23\\\hline 34\end{array}$

Owl / Soccer Ball
35 campers vote for the Owl nebula, but 33 more vote for Soccer Ball. How many vote for Soccer Ball?
$\begin{array}{r}35\\+33\\\hline 68\end{array}$

Fried Egg / Running Chicken
60 campers vote for the Fried Egg nebula and 38 campers vote for Running Chicken. How many fewer campers vote for Running Chicken than for Fried Egg?
$\begin{array}{r}60\\-38\\\hline 22\end{array}$

Necklace
BONUS: Thirty-six campers vote for the Necklace nebula. Then you and 10 friends also vote for it. How many votes in all would that be?
36 + 11 = 47 people

Brain Box

Word problems have certain hints that tell you which operation you need to do to solve the problem.

Addition Clue Words: total number, in all, altogether

Subtraction Clue Words: how many more/less/fewer, how many are left, the difference

Now add this sticker to your map!

Space Vacation on Para-Dice

Circle the correct past tense verb to use in each sentence.

Dear Seth,
I (had) haved a great vacation! First, my family sitted (sat) under the warm pink sun. Then, we (drank) drinked sweet momo fruit juice and (ate) eated piles of space fries. We also go (went) to a festival and heared (heard) the Para-Dice singers perform their hit song. Every afternoon, flocks of orange birds flied (flew) by. Also, I keeped (kept) a beautiful shell from the blue stone beach. I am sad to leave, but I'm excited to see you at space school in September!
Sabrina

Brain Box

A past-tense verb tells about something that has already happened. You can add d or ed to most verbs to make them past finish. However, the verb is an irregular verb. It doesn't follow the same rules as most regular verbs, you may have to change the whole word.

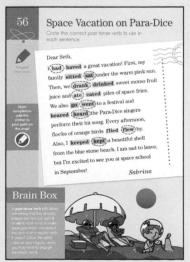

Math Riddle

Add or subtract.

$\begin{array}{r}27\\+27\\\hline 54\end{array}$ G

$\begin{array}{r}56\\+29\\\hline 85\end{array}$ F

$\begin{array}{r}58\\-49\\\hline 9\end{array}$ R

$\begin{array}{r}45\\-19\\\hline 26\end{array}$ P

$\begin{array}{r}35\\+26\\\hline 61\end{array}$ N

$\begin{array}{r}96\\-61\\\hline 35\end{array}$ E

$\begin{array}{r}34\\+37\\\hline 71\end{array}$ O

$\begin{array}{r}82\\+15\\\hline 97\end{array}$ A

$\begin{array}{r}84\\-48\\\hline 36\end{array}$ H

$\begin{array}{r}60\\-32\\\hline 28\end{array}$ L

$\begin{array}{r}74\\+16\\\hline 90\end{array}$ T

Use your answers to decode the riddle.

Riddle:
Why didn't the astronaut take a vacation?

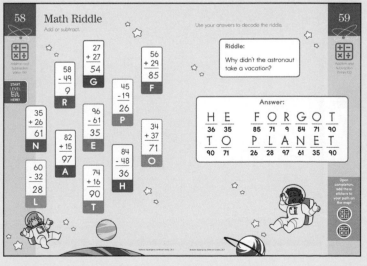

Answer:

H	E		F	O	R	G	O	T
36	35		85	71	9	54	71	90

T	O		P	L	A	N	E	T
90	71		26	28	97	61	35	90

Now add this sticker to your map!

60

Will It Grow?

Read the passage. Then look at each experiment below and answer each question.

You need to eat food to get energy so you can grow. Likewise, plants also need energy to grow, but most plants are able to *make* their own food! They get energy from sunlight and use it, along with air and water, to create their food, called **glucose**. This process is called **photosynthesis**. Plants have a green substance called **chlorophyll** (pronounced *klor-uh-fill*), which uses the light energy from the sun, carbon dioxide from the air, and water from the soil to make glucose.

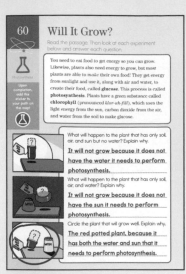

What will happen to the plant that has only soil, air, and sun but no water? Explain why.

It will not grow because it does not have the water it needs to perform photosynthesis.

What will happen to the plant that has only soil, air, and water? Explain why.

It will not grow because it does not have the sun it needs to perform photosynthesis.

Circle the plant that will grow well. Explain why.

The red potted plant, because it has both the water and sun that it needs to perform photosynthesis.

62

Hundreds of Meteors

Add. Then draw a line through your answers to get through the meteor field. (HINT: You may need to regroup.)

Subtract. Then continue the line through your answers to get through the meteor field. (HINT: You may need to regroup.)

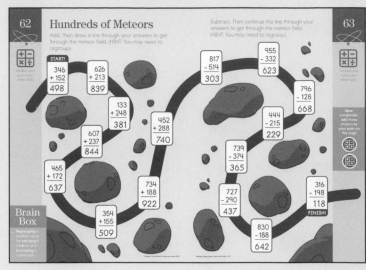

63

START!

$346 + 152 = 498$

$626 + 213 = 839$

$133 + 248 = 381$

$452 + 288 = 740$

$607 + 237 = 844$

$465 + 172 = 637$

$734 + 188 = 922$

$354 + 155 = 509$

$817 - 514 = 303$

$955 - 332 = 623$

$796 - 128 = 668$

$444 - 215 = 229$

$739 - 374 = 365$

$727 - 290 = 437$

$830 - 188 = 642$

$316 - 198 = 118$

FINISH!

Brain Box

Regrouping is another name for carrying in addition and borrowing in subtraction.

Growing Up

Read about the life cycles of butterflies, dogs, and robins. Then answer each question.

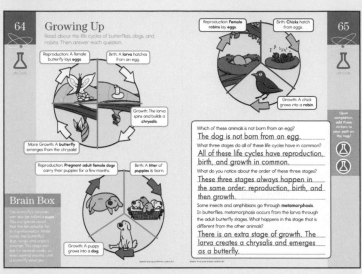

Brain Box

Which of these animals is not born from an egg?

The dog is not born from an egg.

What three stages do all of these life cycles have in common?

All of these life cycles have reproduction, birth, and growth in common.

What do you notice about the order of these three stages?

These three stages always happen in the same order: reproduction, birth, and then growth.

Some insects and amphibians go through **metamorphosis**. In butterflies, metamorphosis occurs from the larva through the adult butterfly stages. What happens in this stage that is different from the other animals?

There is an extra stage of growth. The larva creates a chrysalis and emerges as a butterfly.

Don't Miss the Meteors!

Read each pair of events. One is the **cause** and one is the **effect**. Circle the cause.

67

City parks were full of people excited to see meteors.

(Scientists announced a large meteor shower coming soon.)

Scientists discovered a galaxy far beyond any they had ever seen.

(Scientists built a new, very powerful telescope.)

(A new icy, round object was slightly too small to be a planet.)

Scientists categorized the new satellite as a dwarf planet.

A solar wind blew back the tail of a comet as it shot across the sky.

(The outermost layer of the sun expanded into space, causing a solar wind.)

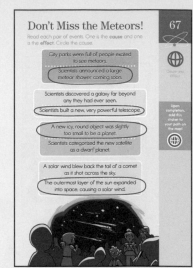

68

Space Plot

Categorize the satellites by length. Make a tally mark in the correct row of the chart for each satellite. Then write the total number of each satellite.

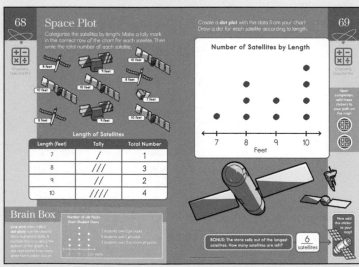

Length of Satellites

Length (feet)	Tally	Total Number
7	/	1
8	///	3
9	//	2
10	////	4

Create a **dot plot** with the data from your chart. Draw a dot for each satellite according to length.

69

Number of Satellites by Length

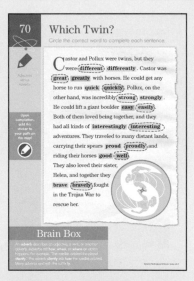

Feet (7, 8, 9, 10)

BONUS: The store sells out of the longest satellites. How many satellites are left?

6 satellites

Brain Box

Line plots (also called **dot plots**) can be used to show numerical data. A number line runs along the bottom of the graph. A dot represents how many times that number occurs.

Number of Jet Packs Each Student Owns:

2 students own 0 jet packs.
4 students own 1 jet pack.
3 students own 2 or more jet packs.

70

Which Twin?

Circle the correct word to complete each sentence.

Castor and Pollux were twins, but they were **different** / **differently**. Castor was **great** / **greatly** with horses. He could get any horse to run **quick** / **quickly**. Pollux, on the other hand, was incredibly **strong** / **strongly**. He could lift a giant boulder **easy** / **easily**. Both of them loved being together, and they had all kinds of **interestingly** / **interesting** adventures. They traveled to many distant lands, carrying their spears **proud** / **proudly** and riding their horses **good** / **well**. They also loved their sister, Helen, and together they **brave** / **bravely** fought in the Trojan War to rescue her.

Brain Box

An **adverb** describes an adjective, a verb, or another adverb. Adverbs tell how, when, or where an action happens. For example, *The castle orbited the planet slowly.* Many adverbs end with the suffix *-ly*.

Out-of-This-World Words

Read the definitions of each word.

behave
verb be·have \bi-'hāv, bē-\
: to act in an acceptable way: to act properly
: to act in a particular way

create
verb cre·ate \krē-'āt, 'krē-\
: to make or produce (something): to cause (something new) to exist
: to cause (a particular situation) to exist

happy
adjective hap·py \'ha-pē\
: feeling pleasure and enjoyment because of your life, situation, etc.
: showing or causing feelings of pleasure and enjoyment

power
noun pow·er \'pau̇(-ə)r\
: the ability or right to control people or things
: political control of a country or area

tell
verb \'tel\
: to say or write (something) to (someone)
: to give information to (someone) by speaking or writing

Choose a prefix to add to each root word to create a new word. Then write the definition of the new word.

re- pre- tell
retell: tell again

super- dis- power
superpower: incredible power

un- mis- happy
unhappy: not happy

co- un- create
cocreate: create together

mis- pre- behave
misbehave: behave badly

Who Made It?

Circle each man-made object. Cross out each natural object.

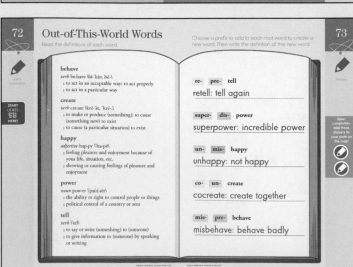

planet Earth
stars in sky
hill in background
flag
landing vehicle
an astronaut suit
rocks in foreground
rover

Brain Box

Natural objects are objects found in the environment, like rocks, water, and trees. Objects created by humans that do our own nature or the environment are man-made. These include roads, machines, and even hamburgers!

Name a man-made object that you might bring to the moon, and explain why you would bring it.

Answers will vary.

A Capital Idea

Circle the letters that should be capitalized in this tourist brochure.

welcome to the capital city of planet purple!

You're just in time for the plum parade.

viola violet, our mayor, will lead us down plum street.

The purple posse will play music for dancing.

Plenty of people will be eating plum pudding–brand ice pops.

kids on floats will throw piles of prizes into the crowds at magenta square.

rick and ronda lavender will broadcast the show on channel 5, purple tv.

When the parade ends at orchid park, there'll be plenty of delicious eggplant for everyone!

BONUS: Imagine a planet where the only color you see is your favorite color. Name and write about your planet using correct capitalization.

Answers will vary.

Brain Box

A common noun names any person, place, or thing. A common noun is not capitalized. A proper noun names a specific person, place, or thing, like a country, month, or holiday. A proper noun is capitalized. For example, *Brazil*, *January*, *July*.

76

Space Snacks

Each graph has a different way of showing the same data. Study the graphs and answer each question about the space snacks.

CRACKERS   COOKIES   CHEESE

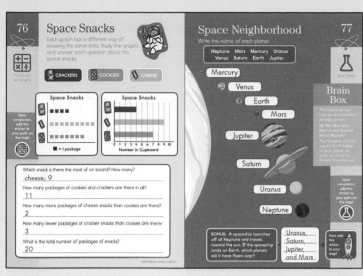

Space Snacks

■ = 1 package

Space Snacks

Number In Cupboard

Which snack is there the most of on board? How many?
cheese; 9

How many packages of cookies and crackers are there in all?
11

How many more packages of cheese snacks than cookies are there?
2

How many fewer packages of cracker snacks than cookies are there?
3

What is the total number of packages of snacks?
20

Space Neighborhood

77

Write the name of each planet.

Neptune Mars Mercury Uranus
Venus Saturn Earth Jupiter

Mercury
Venus
Earth
Mars
Jupiter
Saturn
Uranus
Neptune

Brain Box

The mnemonic can help you to remember all eight planets:

My Very Eloquent Mother Just Served Under Neptune!

The first letter of each word is the first letter of each planet—in order of closest to farthest from the sun.

BONUS: A spaceship launches off of Neptune and travels toward the sun. If the spaceship lands on Earth, which planets will it have flown over?
Uranus, Saturn, Jupiter, and Mars

78

Star System

Write each word from the boxes in the constellation that has the same vowel sound. Now add two words of your own.

perch flew gray birch clue
me space speech coin moon

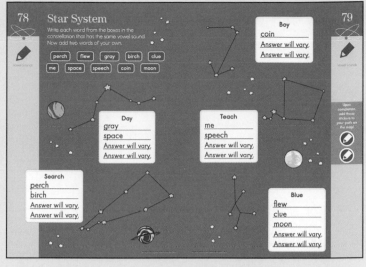

Boy
coin
Answer will vary.
Answer will vary.

Day
gray
space
Answer will vary.
Answer will vary.

Teach
me
speech
Answer will vary.
Answer will vary.

Search
perch
birch
Answer will vary.
Answer will vary.

Blue
flew
clue
moon
Answer will vary.
Answer will vary.

Research It!

Read each research question about the planet of Watoxi, then write where you would look to find the answer.

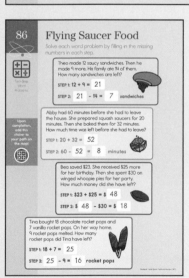

Map   Photograph of emperor   Newspaper
Internet   Biography

What is the life story of Watoxi's most important scientist?
Biography or Internet

What news articles were published on the first day of the big Watoxi war?
Newspaper or Internet

How far is Watoxi's biggest city from the Bubbling Watoxi Sea?
Map or Internet

What did the Watoxi emperor wear on the day he took office?
Photograph of emperor or Internet

What did the Watoxi people write online about the Spacefruit Festival?
Internet

81

Read the news profile. Then answer each question using complete sentences.

Who Is Watoxi's Emperor?

Watoxi's emperor is only seven years old, but he's already made many changes to the planet. A great lover of dogs, he owns twelve of them and has created dog parks all around Watoxi City. He's also installed a roller coaster on the palace grounds, which anyone can ride, free of charge. But he's also capable of serious business. Although his father was never able to work out a treaty with Toboxi, Watoxi's new emperor was able to make an agreement with them—after taking the Toboxi emperor on his roller coaster.

Does the emperor like dogs? Use two details from the text as evidence for your answer.
Yes, because the emperor owns twelve dogs and he builds dog parks around the city.

What two details from the article are illustrated in the pictures?
The emperor likes dogs and roller coasters.

Name two key details that you learn from the text that are **not** illustrated in the pictures.
The emperor built dog parks around the city, and the emperor worked out a treaty with Toboxi.

82

Spacewalks

Solve each word problem by finding the unknown number.

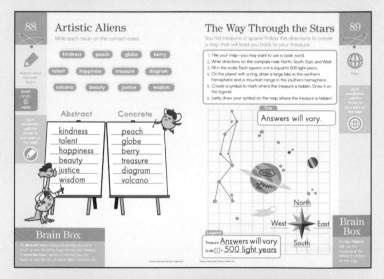

The blue astronaut walked in space for 91 minutes. The next day he spacewalked for another 98 minutes. How many minutes in all were his two walks?
189 minutes

The purple astronaut spacewalked for 370 minutes. The next day she spacewalked again. If she walked for 480 minutes in total, how many minutes did she walk on the second day?
110 minutes

The green astronaut's first spacewalk was 120 minutes long. The second spacewalk was shorter. The total number of minutes for the walks was 200 minutes. How long was his second spacewalk?
80 minutes

According to the information above, how many minutes shorter was the green astronaut's first spacewalk than the purple astronaut's first spacewalk?
250 minutes

Secrets in Stars

Write the names on the correct constellation.

Canis Major (The Great Dog)   Pisces (The Fish)   Gemini (The Twins)
Capricorn (The Sea Goat)   Cygnus (The Swan)   Leo (The Lion)

Leo (The Lion)
Capricornus (The Sea Goat)
Canis Major (The Great Dog)
Cygnus (The Swan)
Pisces (The Fish)
Gemini (The Twins)

Brain Box

A constellation is a group of stars that create a picture in the sky and can look like a person, object, or animal. Try spotting one of the constellations shown above the next time you're outside at night.

Flying Saucer Food

Solve each word problem by filling in the missing numbers in each step.

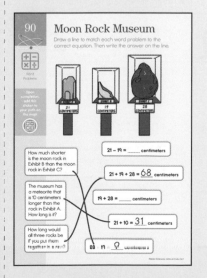

Theo made 12 saucy sandwiches. Then he made 9 more. His family ate 14 of them. How many sandwiches are left?
STEP 1: 12 + 9 = 21
STEP 2: 21 - 14 = 7 sandwiches

Abby had 60 minutes before she had to leave the house. She prepared squash saucers for 20 minutes. Then she baked them for 32 minutes. How much time was left before she had to leave?
STEP 1: 20 + 32 = 52
STEP 2: 60 - 52 = 8 minutes

Bea saved $23. She received $25 more for her birthday. Then she spent $30 on winged whoopie pies for her party. How much money did she have left?
STEP 1: $23 + $25 = $ 48
STEP 2: $ 48 - $30 = $ 18

Tina bought 18 chocolate rocket pops and 7 vanilla rocket pops. On her way home, 9 rocket pops melted. How many rocket pops did Tina have left?
STEP 1: 18 + 7 = 25
STEP 2: 25 - 9 = 16 rocket pops

Artistic Aliens

Write each noun on the correct easel.

kindness peach globe berry
talent happiness treasure diagram
volcano beauty justice wisdom

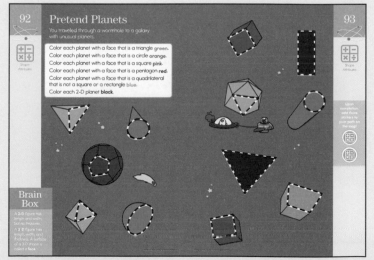

Abstract
kindness
talent
happiness
beauty
justice
wisdom

Concrete
peach
globe
berry
treasure
diagram
volcano

Brain Box

An abstract noun names something you can't touch or see, like ideas, experiences, and feelings. A concrete noun names something you can touch or see, like any physical object around you.

The Way Through the Stars

You hid treasure in space! Follow the directions to create a map that will lead you back to your treasure.

1. Title your map—you may want to use a code word.
2. Write directions on the compass rose: North, South, East, and West.
3. Fill in the scale: Each square unit is equal to 500 light-years.
4. On the planet with a ring, draw a large lake in the northern hemisphere and a mountain range in the southern hemisphere.
5. Create a symbol to mark where the treasure is hidden. Draw it on the legend.
6. Lastly, draw your symbol on the map where the treasure is hidden!

Title
Answers will vary.

North
West   East
South

Legend
Treasure Answers will vary.
Scale 1 : 500 light years

Brain Box

A map's legend tells you the meaning of the different symbols on the map.

Moon Rock Museum

Draw a line to match each word problem to the correct equation. Then write the answer on the line.

31 CENTIMETERS   19 CENTIMETERS   28 CENTIMETERS

How much shorter is the moon rock in Exhibit B than the moon rock in Exhibit C?
21 - 19 = _____ centimeters

The museum has a meteorite that is 10 centimeters longer than the rock in Exhibit A. How long is it?
21 + 19 + 28 = 68 centimeters

How long would all three rocks be if you put them together in a row?
19 + 28 = _____ centimeters

21 + 10 = 31 centimeters

28 - 19 = _____ centimeters

Pretend Planets

You traveled through a wormhole to a galaxy with unusual planets.

Color each planet with a face that is a triangle green.
Color each planet with a face that is a circle orange.
Color each planet with a face that is a square pink.
Color each planet with a face that is a pentagon red.
Color each planet with a face that is a quadrilateral that is not a square or a rectangle blue.
Color each 2-D planet black.

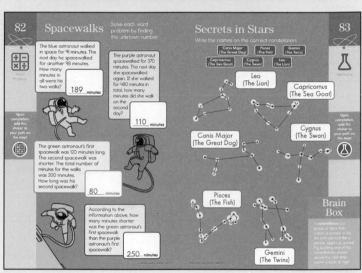
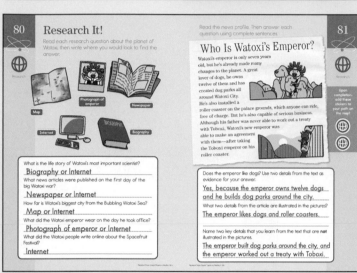

Brain Box

A 2-D figure has length and width but no thickness. A 3-D figure has length, width, and thickness. A surface of a 3-D shape is called a face.

94 Legends of the Milky Way

Read the legends about the creation of the Milky Way. Then answer each question.

Reading Comprehension

A Khoisan legend from Africa claims that the sky was once pure black. The story explains that a lonely girl wanted to visit other people, but there was no light to guide her. So she threw embers into the sky to create the Milky Way to light her path.

A Chinese legend says that a goddess created the Milky Way. When her daughter fell in love with a boy, the goddess became angry. She used a pin to draw a silver line between the lovers so that they would be separated forever, and it became the Milky Way.

A Cherokee legend says the Milky Way was created by a dog who wanted some cornmeal. When he stole a bag, he was chased away. The trail of cornmeal that spilled as he ran created the Milky Way.

Brain Box

The **Milky Way** is the galaxy we live in. A **galaxy** is a system of millions or even billions of stars, gas, and dust that are held together by gravity.

Which story has an animal as the main character?
The Cherokee legend

Who are the main female characters in the stories?
The lonely girl, the angry goddess, and a daughter in love

Which two stories involve scattering something in the sky?
The Khoisan and Cherokee stories

95

According to the Khoisan story, how can the Milky Way help people?
The embers scattered in the sky provide light to guide people in the dark.

In one of the stories, the Milky Way was created by accident. How did this happen?
In the Cherokee story, a dog created the Milky Way by accident by spilling stolen cornmeal.

Choose two legends and write two ways they are alike and two ways they are different.
Answers will vary.

Write and draw your own legend about how the Milky Way was formed! Include at least one feature to make it similar to the legends and one feature to make it different.
Answers will vary.

Upon completion, add these stickers to your path on the map!

96 Save or Spend?

Read the passage. Then answer each question.

Economics

Ido has been saving up to buy a new jet pack that costs 30 space bucks. Ido's mom gives him 3 space bucks a week for his allowance. Ido can earn 2 more space bucks per week by collecting space rocks around the neighborhood. But he loves buying solar snacks on his way home from school. They cost 1 space buck each.

What does Ido have to choose **not** to have if he wants to buy the jet pack sooner?
Ido should choose not to buy solar snacks.

If Ido buys a solar snack every week, what is the consequence?
It will take him longer to save up for the jet pack.

What can Ido do to earn extra space bucks?
Ido can collect rocks around his neighborhood.

What is the fastest way for Ido to save 30 space bucks?
To not buy any snacks, and to collect rocks every week.

If a jet pack costs the same amount as 30 snacks, which would you rather have, and why?
Answers will vary.

BONUS: If you wanted to earn money to take a trip to a constellation, what could you do to make and save money?
Answers will vary.

Upon completion, add this sticker to your path on the map! Now add this sticker to your map!

97 Past, Present, and Future

Choose the correct verbs to complete the fable.

Verb Tenses

Once upon a time, a miser (hid) hides his gold at the foot of a tree in a biosphere (a special zone for living things). But he (didn't leave) will leave it there. Every week, he digs (dug) it up, just to look at it.

But the old miser wasn't the only one who looks (looked) at his gold. One day, a thief will see (saw) him with it! So the thief came back and steals (stole) it all.

When the old miser discovered his gold was gone, he made such a ruckus that all his neighbors will come (came) outside.

"Did you ever use the gold?" one asked him.

"No," he said. "I only looked at it."

"Then look at the hole that the thief left," the neighbor said. "It will do you just as much good."

Brain Box

The **past tense** describes things that already happened, the **present tense** describes things that are happening now, and the **future tense** describes things that will happen.

Upon completion, add this sticker to your path on the map!

98 Can It Be Reversed?

Look at each picture, and write whether the situation is **reversible** or **irreversible**.

Reversible and Irreversible Changes

- ice on wings: reversible
- melted metal: reversible
- mixed paint: irreversible
- thick mist on windows: reversible

Brain Box

If a change can be undone, it is called a **reversible change**. For example, ice can melt, then freeze again. But if the change cannot be undone, it is called an **irreversible change**. For example, if you cook an egg, the egg cannot be uncooked.

99

- melted popsicle: reversible
- steam: reversible
- toasted bread: irreversible

BONUS: An ice-covered asteroid orbits close to the sun and then far from the sun. What reversible change could happen? Explain your answer.
The ice could melt because of the sun's heat and then refreeze when the asteroid is far from the sun.

Upon completion, add these stickers to your path on the map! Now add this sticker to your map!

100 Deep Space Snacks

Draw a line to split the fruit snack in half. Then write the number name for one part.

Fractions

$\frac{1}{2}$ $\frac{1}{2}$

Answers will vary.

Draw two lines to split the snack in thirds. Then write the number name for one part.

$\frac{1}{3}$

Brain Box

Fractions show parts of a whole. They can be written in words (one-half) or as a figure ($\frac{1}{2}$).

101

Draw two or three lines to split each snack into fourths. Then write the number name for one part.

$\frac{1}{4}$ $\frac{1}{4}$ $\frac{1}{4}$

Draw your favorite food. Divide it into fourths and write the fraction for one part.

Answers will vary. $\frac{1}{4}$

Upon completion, add these stickers to your path on the map!

102 Paul Bunyan in Space

Read the story. Then answer each question with complete sentences.

Characters

Paul Bunyan was a giant of a man who had already accomplished a lot on Earth. When he couldn't find a watering hole big enough for his best friend, Babe the Blue Ox, he dug five new ones: the Great Lakes. One day, when he needed to put out a fire, he piled rocks on the cinders and created Mount Hood in Oregon. But it had been a long time since those adventures, and he was looking for a new challenge.

So when the first rocket was ready to be shot into space, the president called Paul. "We want to see what it's like out there in space," the president told him. "Will you hitch a ride on our rocket and take a look around?" So when the rocket was launched into space, Paul was hanging on. "I'm glad you're here," the Man in the Moon said when Paul arrived in space. "I've got an itch that I can't scratch, because I don't have any hands. Can you help me?" At first Paul tried to use a feather from the tail of the Swan constellation, but that only made the Moon giggle. Meanwhile, Babe had been making friends with the Ram. "Here, use my horn," the Ram said. So Paul picked him up, horns and all, and used him to scratch the Moon's nose. Along the way, the Ram's horns dug some holes in the moon. And that's how the Moon got its craters.

Brain Box

A **folktale** is a story that people pass on by telling it over and over again. It isn't written by a single author.

103

What did the president do to find out what's in space?
The president called Paul and asked him to go on a rocket to space.

Why do you think Paul Bunyan accepted the president's challenge?
Sample answer: Paul was adventurous, hardworking, and helpful.

What did the Man in the Moon do when his nose became itchy?
The Man in the Moon asked Paul for help with his itchy nose.

What was Paul's first solution to this challenge?
Paul tried to use a feather from the Swan constellation to scratch the Moon's nose.

What did Paul do when his first idea didn't work out?
Paul tried again and used the Ram's horn to scratch the Moon's nose.

BONUS: Paul Bunyan next meets Andromeda, a princess and constellation. She is chained to the sky and wants to be free. Based on the story above, do you think Paul Bunyan would help her? Make a prediction and write a short story.
Answers will vary.

Upon completion, add these stickers to your path on the map! Now add this sticker to your map!

104 Rows and Columns

Count the number in each row. Then fill in the missing numbers to find the total.

Equal Groups: Arrays

How many rovers are there? 2 + 2 + 2 = 6 rovers

How many space aliens are there? 3 + 3 + 3 + 3 + 3 = 15 space aliens

How many comets are there? 5 + 5 + 5 = 15 comets

How many rockets are there? 4 + 4 + 4 + 4 = 16 rockets

How many telescopes are there? 6 + 6 = 12 telescopes

Upon completion, add this sticker to your path on the map!

106 Star Clusters

Count the number of equal groups. Fill in the missing numbers to find the products.

Equal Groups

2 groups of 6 = 12; 2 x 6 = 12

3 groups of 7 = 21; 3 x 7 = 21

5 groups of 6 = 30; 5 x 6 = 30

6 groups of 4 = 24; 6 x 4 = 24

7 groups of 4 = 28; 7 x 4 = 28

Brain Box

The multiplication symbol (x) means join equal groups.

107 Planet Pops

Divide these planet pops equally. Draw circles to make equal groups. Then solve each equation.

Share 16 Earth pops equally among 2 people. How many pops does each person get? 16 ÷ 2 = 8 pops

Share 30 Saturn pops equally among 5 people. How many pops does each person get? 30 ÷ 5 = 6 pops

Share 20 Venus pops equally among 5 people. How many pops does each person get? 20 ÷ 5 = 4 pops

Share 21 Jupiter pops equally among 7 people. How many pops does each person get? 21 ÷ 7 = 3 pops

Share 18 Mercury pops equally among 3 people. How many pops does each person get? 18 ÷ 3 = 6 pops

Brain Box

The division symbol (÷) means separate into equal groups.

Upon completion, add these stickers to your path on the map!

108 How Did Thor Get His Hammer?

Read this old Norse story. Then answer each question using complete sentences.

Main Idea and Conclusions

Thor was known for his giant hammer. He used it as a weapon and for important ceremonies and blessings. Although the weapon became precious to him, he received it from a trickster named Loki after a few mean tricks.

One day, Loki, the trickster, was in the mood for mischief. So he cut off all the beautiful gold hair of Sif, Thor's wife. Of course, Thor was furious. But when Thor grabbed Loki, he begged Thor not to hurt him. He offered to go ask the dwarfs, who could make anything, to make more hair for Sif. Thor agreed, so Loki set off for the land of the dwarfs.

Sure enough, the dwarf Ivaldi fashioned a new head of hair for Sif. But he didn't stop there. He also made a ship that could be folded up and put in a pocket and the world's deadliest spear.

But Loki wasn't satisfied with these incredible gifts. So he taunted two other dwarf craftsmen: "I bet *you* can't make anything as good as what Ivaldi just made!" Not to be outdone, those dwarfs began making a golden boar and a gold ring that made new rings. But as they were finishing their creations, Loki realized he was about to lose his bet! So he turned himself into a fly and began to bite the craftsmen in order to distract them.

Brain Box

A **myth** is a traditional story that often explains the early history of a people or a natural wonder. Norse mythology is a collection of tales from ancient Scandinavia, which includes the countries of Denmark, Norway, and Sweden.

109

One of the craftsmen was also working on the best hammer in the world. The hammer never missed when it was thrown, and it came back to its owner like a boomerang when it was done. The hammer was nearly complete when Loki's bite startled the craftsman and he was too hurt to continue. So the handle turned out just a little too short.

Despite the flawed handle, the other dwarf craftsmen proved that they were just as good as Ivaldi because when Thor received the hammer, it became his most prized possession. He realized its power, and from that day on he took it everywhere. And now his hammer is just as famous as he is.

What is the first thing that happens in this story?
The first thing that happens in this story is that Loki cuts Sif's hair.

How does Thor feel about this event? Use a detail from the text that shows his feelings.
Thor is furious that Loki cut Sif's hair. He shows this by grabbing Loki.

Which character speaks the one line of dialogue in this story?
Loki says the one line of dialogue in this story.

What are the dwarfs good at?
Dwarfs are good at making incredible gifts.

What is the main question that this story answers?
The main question is how Thor got his hammer.

What happens at the end of this story?
At the end of this story, Loki is proven wrong and Thor receives a powerful hammer.

Upon completion, add these stickers to your path on the map!

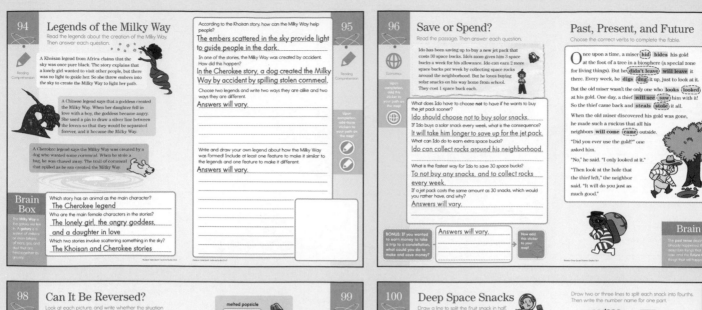

Reading Clues

Draw a line to match each plant or animal to its fossil.

Brain Box

A fossil is the remains, or impression, marks left behind by a prehistoric plant or animal. Plant and animal fossils often occur near rivers, ponds, and lakes. For example, plant parts fall or are washed into bodies of water and become buried under layers of dirt. If more dirt is pressed on top, the pressure will make the fossil's impression.

Write about and draw what fossils this fern may leave in the future.

Answers will vary.

What's the Difference?

Take a look at both pictures. Circle each object in the present that has changed as time passed.

PAST

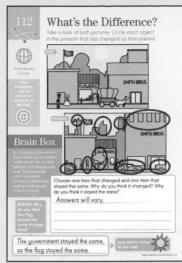

PRESENT

Brain Box

By comparing the past with the present we can better understand how societies behave and change over time. This knowledge can help explain current problems and perhaps lead people to find solutions.

Choose one item that changed and one item that stayed the same. Why do you think it changed? Why do you think it stayed the same?

Answers will vary.

BONUS: Why do you think the flag stayed the same through time?

The government stayed the same, so the flag stayed the same.

Now add this sticker to your map!

Connect the Stars

Complete each sentence with a linking word or phrase from the box.

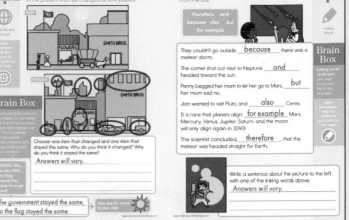

therefore · and · because · also · but · for example

They couldn't go outside __because__ there was a meteor storm.

The comet shot out next to Neptune __and__ headed toward the sun.

Penny begged her mom to let her go to Mars, __but__ her mom said no.

Jian wanted to visit Pluto, and __also__ Ceres.

It is rare that planets align __for example__ Mars, Mercury, Venus, Jupiter, Saturn, and the moon will only align again in 2040!

The scientist concluded, __therefore__, that the meteor was headed straight for Earth.

Brain Box

Linking words or phrases are used to connect two or more ideas.

Write a sentence about the picture to the left with one of the linking words above.

Answers will vary.

Moon Fractions

What part of each moon is shown? Fill in the missing parts of the fraction to answer.

This is $\frac{1}{4}$. What fraction is this? $\frac{2}{4}$

This is $\frac{1}{3}$. What fraction is this? $\frac{2}{3}$

This is $\frac{1}{6}$. What fraction is this? $\frac{3}{6}$

This is $\frac{1}{8}$. What fraction is this? $\frac{4}{8}$

Each part of the moon is $\frac{1}{4}$. Color $\frac{3}{4}$ of the moon.

Planet Peril

Erosion is what happens when wind or water changes the shape of land. Read about how to prevent erosion. Then answer each question.

Dikes
Dikes are walls built to keep the sea from flooding the land. Dikes can be natural or man-made. People often create dikes with sandbags. Sand absorbs water and lets very little water through.

Lightning Rod
A lightning rod is a metal rod attached to a tall building. Lightning will strike the rod and travel down a wire to channel the electricity safely into the ground.

Hedges
A hedge is a group of sturdy plants that form a boundary or fence. The strong plants that form a hedge can block wind and shelter yards.

What can keep an ocean-side city from sinking into the sea? Explain how.
A dike made of sandbags because they are filled with sand that can absorb water.

What can keep a tall building from being damaged during a lightning storm? Explain how.
A lightning rod because it can safely channel the lightning to the ground.

What can protect gardens from wind? Explain how.
A hedge. It has strong plants that can block wind.

Space Junk

Read each word problem. Then draw a picture and write an equation to solve.

Two robots gathered 9 pieces of space junk each. How many pieces of space junk did they have altogether?
$2 \times 9 = 18$
18 pieces

The robots then separated their junk into 3 equal groups. How many pieces were in each group?
$18 \div 3 = 6$
6 pieces

If 6 space dogs were given 5 bones each, what is the total number of bones the dogs were given?
$6 \times 5 = 30$
30 bones

Forty-eight meteors fell to the earth over 8 days. If an equal amount fell each day, how many meteors fell each day?
$48 \div 8 = 6$
6 meteors

Alien Agreement

Circle the word that correctly completes each sentence.

The Tigs and the Tugs never get along at (his / **their**) yearly barbecue. The Tigs think Mr. Tug makes (**his** / their) sauce too spicy. The Tugs think Mrs. Tig adds too much sugar to (her / **their**) lemonade. But (**everybody** / anybody) loves the Tig-Tug ice cream. Mr. Tug knows half of the recipe, and Mrs. Tig has the other half in (her / **their**) head. Nobody could get it (**it** / them) alone, so everyone keeps getting together. "It's delicious!" (**they** / she) all agree.

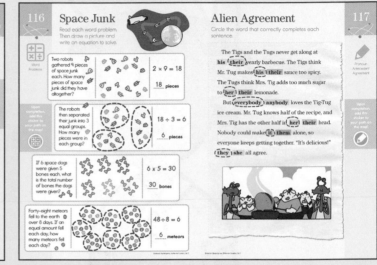

Around the Universe

Each planet takes a different number of days to orbit its star. Round each number of days to the nearest ten.

67 days = 70 days
35 days = 40 days
12 days = 10 days
31 days = 30 days
88 days = 90 days
54 days = 50 days
19 days = 20 days
23 days = 20 days
46 days = 50 days
92 days = 90 days

Round each number of days to the nearest hundred.

373 days = 400 days
406 days = 400 days
159 days = 200 days
555 days = 600 days
836 days = 800 days
490 days = 500 days
225 days = 200 days
777 days = 800 days

Brain Box

To round to the nearest hundred, find the number in the tens place. If the number is 5 or greater, round up. If the number is 4 or less, round down.

Able and Baker were two monkeys who flew to about 360 miles above Earth. Could the exact height be 363 miles? Why or why not?
Yes, because about 360 is a rounded number. 363 becomes 360 when rounded to the nearest ten.

Brain Box

To round to the nearest ten, find the number in the ones place. If the number is 5 or greater, round up. If the number is 4 or less, round down.

CONGRATULATIONS! You completed all of your math quests! You earned:

Which Works Better?

Obi and Tobi each designed a machine to make spaceberry pancakes. Read the data from their breakfast test, and answer each question.

	OBI	TOBI
Pancakes Made per Minute	2	4
Pancakes Burned per Minute	1	3
Cups of Wasted Pancake Batter	2	1
Fluffiness of Pancakes (5 = fluffy, 1 = not fluffy)	5	3

Brain Box

Data is the information you get when you do research or run a test.

Whose machine made the most pancakes per minute?
Tobi

Whose machine wasted the most batter?
Obi

Whose machine burned the most pancakes?
Tobi

Whose machine made the fluffiest pancakes?
Obi

If you throw away the burned pancakes, how many good pancakes did Obi's machine make per minute?
One

If you throw away the burned pancakes, how many good pancakes did Tobi's machine make per minute?
One

Whose machine made the most pancakes that weren't burned, with the least batter wasted?
Tobi

What do you think is a strength of Obi's machine?
Obi's machine made fluffier pancakes and burned fewer pancakes.

What do you think is a strength of Tobi's machine?
Tobi's machine made pancakes more quickly and wasted less batter.

CONGRATULATIONS! You completed all of your science quests! You earned:

Who? What? Where?

Read the fable. Then answer each question.

Country Mouse and City Mouse

One day, City Mouse went to visit his cousin in the country, far from Cosmic City. His cousin, Country Mouse, wasn't fancy, but he loved his city cousin. All Country Mouse had to offer were Big Dipper beans, comet cheese, and potatoes from Pluto, but he offered them freely.

City Mouse turned up his nose at the country fare. "I can't understand how you eat food like this," he said. "But what can you expect in the country? Come to Cosmic City with me! You'll never want to return here."

The two mice set off by rocket for the city and arrived that night.

"You must be hungry after the trip," the City Mouse said. So he took his cousin to a grand dining room. They found the remains of a feast, and dined on moon pie crumbs and space jam.

Suddenly, they heard growling and barking.

"What is that?" asked Country Mouse.

"It is only the dogs of the house," City Mouse told him.

"Only!" said Country Mouse. "I do *not* like that as music during dinner."

The door to the dining room flew open. Two giant space dogs dashed in.

City Mouse and Country Mouse scrambled to escape.

"Good-bye, Cousin," Country Mouse said.

"Are you going so soon?" City Mouse asked.

"Yes," Country Mouse said. "Better beans and potatoes in peace than moon pies in fear."

Who visited Country Mouse?
City Mouse

What did Country Mouse serve City Mouse to eat?
Big Dipper beans, comet cheese, and potatoes

Where did City Mouse and Country Mouse go together?
To the city

When did they arrive?
The same night

Why did City Mouse think Country Mouse would like the city?
The food was better there.

How did Country Mouse and City Mouse realize there were dogs nearby?
They heard growling and barking.

What did Country Mouse mean when he said, "Better beans and potatoes in peace than moon pies in fear?"
Answers will vary. Better to live a simple life in peace than to have fancy things and be in danger.

BONUS: Imagine that City Mouse takes Country Mouse on a helicopter ride over Cosmic City. Write a few sentences to describe where they might go and what they might see.

Answers will vary.

The Space Age Begins

Read about the space race. Then write the title of each event and the date in the correct place on the timeline below.

SPUTNIK 1
On October 4, 1957, the former Soviet Union sent *Sputnik 1* into orbit. It was the first man-made satellite (a satellite can be any object in orbit around a planet—in fact, our moon is a natural satellite). The success of *Sputnik 1* started the "Space Race"—a race between the Soviet Union and the United States to be the first to put a man on the moon.

SPUTNIK 2
The Soviet Union launched *Sputnik 2* soon after, on November 3, 1957—this time, with a dog named Laika inside! This was the first satellite to carry a life-form. Meanwhile, the U.S. hadn't yet launched a thing.

EXPLORER 1
On January 31, 1958, the Americans began to catch up in the space race. With a slight delay, they not only reached orbit, but also gathered useful scientific information.

NASA
President Dwight Eisenhower announced a new government-run agency that would explore space. On July 29, 1958, the National Aeronautics and Space Administration (NASA) was born!

LUNA 1
The Soviets nearly reached the moon on January 2, 1959, with their spacecraft *Luna 1*. However, it missed its mark! As a result, it was the first spacecraft to leave the orbit of Earth.

LUNA 2
Luna 2 was the first spacecraft to successfully reach the moon's surface. It took around 34 hours to get there, and crash-landed on September 14, 1959. Luckily, no one was inside! The Soviets were still in the lead.

FIRST MAN IN SPACE
Yuri Gagarin became the first man in space on April 12, 1961. His spacecraft, *Vostok 1*, circled around the earth and landed about two hours after it had launched. Gagarin parachuted out of his spacecraft before it crash-landed.

FIRST WOMAN IN SPACE
Just two years later, on June 16, 1963, Valentina Tereshkova became the first woman in space.

A MAN ON THE MOON
It wasn't until six years later that the U.S. was able to land a man on the moon. On July 20, 1969, *Apollo 11* landed, and Neil Armstrong became the first man to walk on the moon. The U.S. had won the space race!

Explorer 1, January 31, 1958
Sputnik 1, October 4, 1957
Sputnik 2, November 3, 1957
NASA, July 29, 1958
Luna 2, September 14, 1959
Luna 1, January 2, 1959
First Man in Space, April 12, 1961
First Woman in Space, June 16, 1963
A Man on the Moon, July 20, 1969

1955   1960   1965   1970

CONGRATULATIONS! You completed all of your social studies quests! You earned:

Summer Brain Quest Extras

Stay smart all summer long with these Summer Brain Quest Extras! In this section you'll find:

Summer Brain Quest Reading List

A book can take you anywhere—and summer is a great time to go on a reading adventure! Use the Summer Brain Quest Reading List to help you start the next chapter of your quest!

Summer Brain Quest Mini Deck

Cut out the cards and make your own Summer Brain Quest Mini Deck. Play by yourself or with a friend.

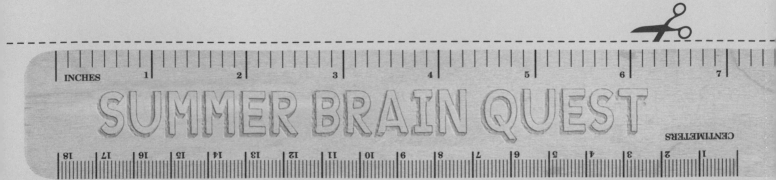

INCHES 1 2 3 4 5 6 7

SUMMER BRAIN QUEST

CENTIMETERS
18 17 16 15 14 13 12 11 10 9 8 7 6 5 4 3 2 1

Summer Brain Quest
Reading List

We recommend reading at least 15 to 30 minutes each day. Read to yourself or aloud. You can also read aloud with a friend or family member and discuss the book. Here are some questions to get you started:

- **Was the book a nonfiction (informational) or fiction (story/narrative) text?**
- **Who or what was the book about?**
- **What was the setting of the story (where did it take place)?**
- **Was there a main character? Who was it? Describe the character.**
- **Was there a problem in the story? What was it? How was it solved?**
- **Were there any themes in the story? What were they? How do you know?**
- **Were there any lessons in the story? What were they? How do you know?**
- **Why do you think the author wrote the book?**

Jump-start your reading adventure by visiting your local library or bookstore and checking out the following books. Track which ones you've read, and write your own review! Would you recommend this book to a friend? If so, which friend would you recommend this book to, and why?

Fiction

Charlotte's Web, written by E. B. White, illustrated by Garth Williams

Wilbur the pig was born the runt of his litter, and the farmer thinks he's due for slaughter. Luckily his spider friend Charlotte has a clever, web-spinning plan that just might save his life!

DATE STARTED: _____   DATE FINISHED: _____

MY REVIEW: _____

_____

The Day the Crayons Quit, written by Drew Daywalt, illustrated by Oliver Jeffers

Duncan's crayons are on strike. Black is sick of outlining, and blue is tired from filling in all those oceans. How can Duncan get the crayons to color for him again?

DATE STARTED: _____   DATE FINISHED: _____

MY REVIEW: _____

_____

Flat Stanley (Flat Stanley Series, No. 1), written by Jeff Brown, illustrated by Macky Pamintuan

When a bulletin board flattens Stanley to half an inch thick, he discovers that flatness has its benefits. Not only can he be flown like a kite, but he can also help catch criminals!

DATE STARTED: _____   DATE FINISHED: _____

MY REVIEW: _____

_____

If You Decide to Go to the Moon, written by Faith McNulty, illustrated by Steven Kellogg

If you dream of being an astronaut, look no further than this nifty guide to space travel!

DATE STARTED: _____   DATE FINISHED: _____

MY REVIEW: _____

_____

Frightlopedia: An Encyclopedia of Everything Scary, Creepy, and Spine-Chilling, from Arachnids to Zombies, written by Julie Winterbottom, illustrated by Stefano Tambellini

Love scary stuff? This book has everything from ghost stories to gruesome creatures to scary science. Keep your flashlight handy!

DATE STARTED: _____   DATE FINISHED: _____

MY REVIEW: _____

_____

Junie B. Jones and the Stupid Smelly Bus (Junie B. Jones Series, No. 1), written by Barbara Park, illustrated by Denise Brunkus

Junie B. Jones is so scared of riding the bus that she hides in a supply closet on her first day of school. And that's just the beginning of her laugh-out-loud adventure.

DATE STARTED: _____   DATE FINISHED: _____

MY REVIEW: _____

_____

Marisol McDonald Doesn't Match, written by Monica Brown, illustrated by Sara Palacios

Marisol likes unique combinations—PB&J on burritos, polka-dot shirts with striped pants, and her own red hair and brown skin, which come from her Scottish and Peruvian roots.

DATE STARTED: _____   DATE FINISHED: _____

MY REVIEW: _____

_____

Midnight on the Moon (Magic Treehouse Series, No. 8), written by Mary Pope Osborne, illustrated by Sal Murdocca

Join siblings Jack and Annie on their space adventure as they travel 40 years into the future!

DATE STARTED: _____   DATE FINISHED: _____

MY REVIEW: _____

_____

My Name Is Sangoel, written by Karen Lynn Williams and Khadra Mohammed, illustrated by Catherine Stock

Sangoel is a refugee from Sudan. He misses home; no one in America can pronounce his name, but he refuses to change it. One day, he comes up with a creative solution. . . .

DATE STARTED: _____   DATE FINISHED: _____

MY REVIEW: _____

_____

The Search for the Slimy Space Slugs! (Doodle Adventures No. 1), written and illustrated by Mike Lowery

Carl the duck is a member of a super-secret international group of explorers. Join him on an important journey through space—and don't forget to add your very own doodles!

DATE STARTED: _____   DATE FINISHED: _____

MY REVIEW: _____

_____

Nonfiction

Eye to Eye: How Animals See the World, written and illustrated by Steve Jenkins

The first animal eye didn't look very much like an eye at all; it was just a clump of light-sensitive cells. But now the eyes of animals come in many varieties, from pinholes to cameras. See them up close!

DATE STARTED: _____ DATE FINISHED: _____

MY REVIEW: _____

_____

The History of Counting, written by Denise Schmandt-Besserat, illustrated by Michael Hays

How did people count before they had numbers? In this book, you'll learn all about the different counting systems around the world that use everything from body parts to pebbles!

DATE STARTED: _____ DATE FINISHED: _____

MY REVIEW: _____

_____

How Come? Every Kid's Science Questions Explained, written by Kathy Wollard, illustrated by Debra Solomon

If the earth is spinning, why can't we feel it? Find the answer to this question and many more in this fun science book!

DATE STARTED: _____ DATE FINISHED: _____

MY REVIEW: _____

_____

How Big Were Dinosaurs?, written and illustrated by Lita Judge

Even though dinosaurs went extinct 65 million years ago, we know how big they were from fossils of their bones. How do they compare to animals that roam the earth today?

DATE STARTED: _____ DATE FINISHED: _____

MY REVIEW: _____

_____

Moonshot: The Flight of Apollo 11, written and illustrated by Brian Floca

This is the story of the first time that humans landed on the moon—from the moment of blastoff to Neil Armstrong's first footsteps on the moon's surface.

DATE STARTED: _____ DATE FINISHED: _____

MY REVIEW: _____

_____

Our Solar System, by Seymour Simon

Did you know that if the sun were hollow, it could hold 1.3 million Earths? Read this book to find out more about our fascinating solar system!

DATE STARTED: _____ DATE FINISHED: _____

MY REVIEW: _____

_____

She Loved Baseball: The Effa Manley Story, written by Audrey Vernick, illustrated by Don Tate

Effa Manley was the first—and only—woman to be inducted into the Baseball Hall of Fame. Read about her love of the game and her heroic fight for equal treatment.

DATE STARTED: _____   DATE FINISHED: _____

MY REVIEW: _____

_____

Sixteen Years in Sixteen Seconds: The Sammy Lee Story, written by Paula Yoo, illustrated by Dom Lee

Despite the discrimination he faced, diver Sammy Lee trained for 16 years to become the first Asian American to win an Olympic gold medal.

DATE STARTED: _____   DATE FINISHED: _____

MY REVIEW: _____

_____

The Book of Totally Irresponsible Science: 64 Daring Experiments for Young Scientists, written by Sean Connolly

From Homemade Lightning to a Giant Air Cannon, you can demonstrate scientific principles that pop, crackle, ooze, boom, and even stink!

DATE STARTED: _____   DATE FINISHED: _____

MY REVIEW: _____

_____

A Splash of Red: The Life and Art of Horace Pippin, written by Jen Bryant, illustrated by Melissa Sweet

Ever since he was little, Horace Pippin loved drawing. He wouldn't even let a war wound stop him, and instead used painting to strengthen his injured arm after serving in World War I.

DATE STARTED: _____   DATE FINISHED: _____

MY REVIEW: _____

_____

And don't stop here! There's a whole world to discover. All you need is a book!

Summer Brain Quest Mini Deck

QUESTIONS

 There are three hundred twenty-six minutes until a rocket blasts off. Write the number in standard form.

 Is a book made up of chapters, or is a chapter made up of books?

 True or false: You can tell the difference between water and steam just by looking at them.

 Is the American flag flown at the top or bottom of the pole?

QUESTIONS

 The weather station launched 25 blue weather balloons and 43 red weather balloons. How many weather balloons were launched in all?

 Where should a conclusion be placed in an essay?

 What would be a stronger material for building a bridge, steel or rope?

 True or false: A map can tell you what is north and what is south, but not how far one city is from another.

QUESTIONS

 One moon rock is 5 inches long. Another is 2 inches long. What is the difference in length of the two moon rocks?

 What do you call more than one child?

 True or false: Dogs need to be pollinated in order to make puppies.

 Which is longer, a decade or a century?

QUESTIONS

 Your model rocket stays in the air for 85 seconds. How many seconds is that rounded to the nearest ten?

 What is the superlative of good—**better** or **best**?

 Would a tree that grows on land be able to grow just as well under water?

 True or false: Native Americans lived in North and South America before Europeans arrived.

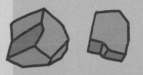

ANSWERS

 68

 at the end

 steel

 false

ANSWERS

 326

 A book is made up of chapters.

 true

 top

ANSWERS

 90

 best

 no

 true

ANSWERS

 3 inches

 children

 false

a century

QUESTIONS

 Your pilot training class begins at 9:25 a.m. What number will the minute hand on the clock point to at that time?

 What does the prefix **re-** mean?

 True or false: A dike is a structure that keeps a city from being flooded by water.

 Are things that happen in cities called **urban** or **suburban**?

QUESTIONS

 If you count by tens, what are the next five numbers?
10, 20, 30, 40, 50, 60,
70, 80, 90, 100, . . .

 Is the **a** sound in **day** a long or short vowel?

 Does it take **years** or **centuries** for a river to create a canyon?

 What animal is important in many Native American stories about the creation of the world?

QUESTIONS

 How many dimes do you need to buy an astronaut figure that costs 80¢?

 Who was Paul Bunyan's best friend?

 True or false: A map shows only land, but not the oceans.

 True or false: A compass rose tells you how far away things are from each other.

QUESTIONS

 What is the digit in the hundreds place of 459?

 Does **beach** rhyme with **speech**?

 True or false: Plants need only sun or water, not both.

 True or false: Human beings can't change something as big as a mountain or an ocean.

ANSWERS

 110, 120, 130, 140, 150

 a long vowel

 centuries

 a turtle

ANSWERS

 the 5

 again

 true

 urban

ANSWERS

 4

 yes

 false

 false

ANSWERS

 8

 Babe the Blue Ox

 false

 false

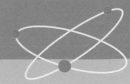

159

QUESTIONS

 A full moon is divided into 2 equal parts. What is the name for one of the parts?

 True or false: A noun is a word used to describe an action.

 True or false: Most of the water on Earth is frozen.

 True or false: Erosion hasn't changed the way the world looks.

QUESTIONS

 There are 4 rows of 6 seats in the planetarium. How many seats are there in all?

 Which of these is a reflexive pronoun: **me**, **myself**, or **mine**?

 True or false: If a glass jug breaks from the cold, it'll be fine once it warms back up.

 True or false: One person can't make a difference in history.

QUESTIONS

 What solid shape is a satellite that has 6 identical square faces?

 Would you use an almanac or a dictionary if you wanted to know how something was spelled?

 Is burning wood into ashes an example of a reversible or irreversible change?

 If more people want to buy something, will the price of it go up or down?

QUESTIONS

 Two children shared 14 star crackers equally. How many crackers did each child get?

 Which is correct: "The girl ran quick" or "The girl ran quickly"?

 True or false: Wind isn't strong enough to change the shape of land.

 Are stories and paintings part of culture?

ANSWERS

 24

 myself

 false

 false

ANSWERS

 one-half

 false

 false

 false

ANSWERS

 7

 The girl ran quickly.

 false

 yes

ANSWERS

 a cube

 a dictionary

 irreversible change

 up

Level 1

START!

Level 2

Level 3

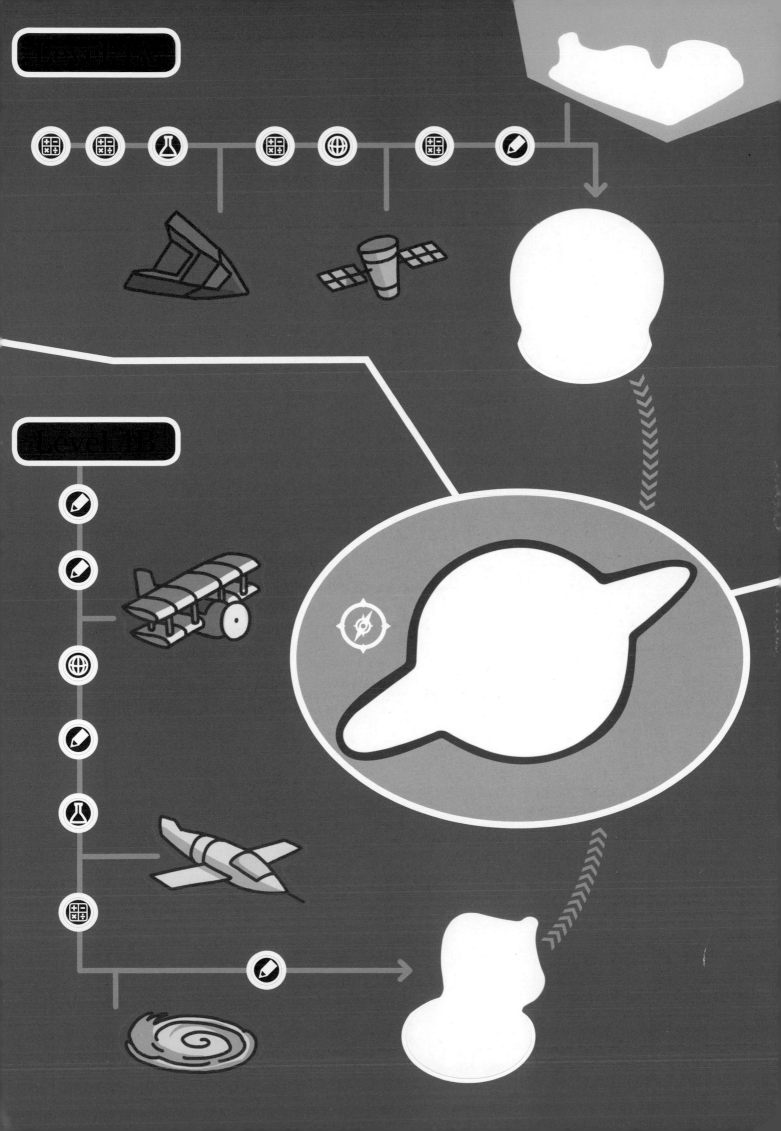

Level 5A

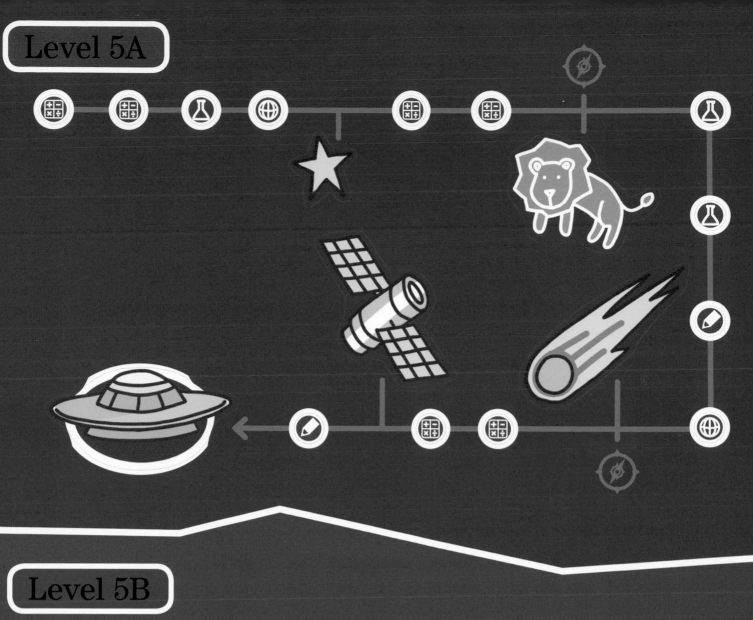

Level 5B

Level 6

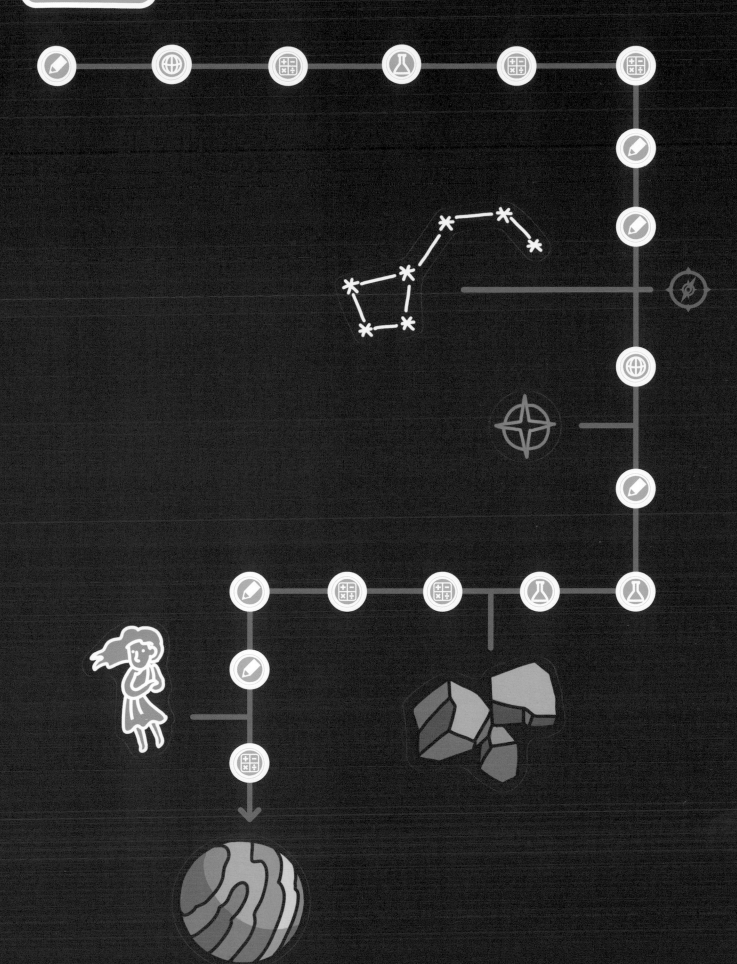

Level 7

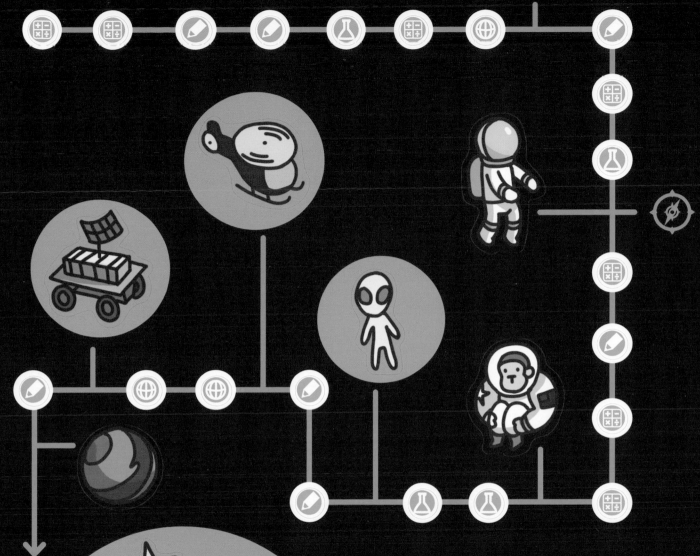

QUEST
complete!
Welcome to
3rd grade!

Did you sticker
every route
possible and
finish **all** the
Outside Quests?
What an achievement!

You've earned the
100% STICKER!